Deep Autumn

short stories

second edition

Also by Michael-Patrick Harrington:

I See No Angels

Saving Magdalene

www.michaelpatrickharrington.com

Deep Autumn

Michael-Patrick Harrington

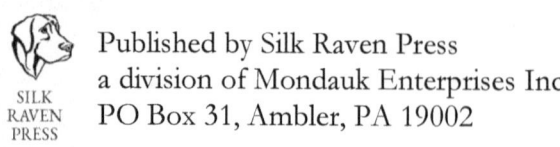

Published by Silk Raven Press
a division of Mondauk Enterprises Inc.
PO Box 31, Ambler, PA 19002

(SRP-001)

ISBN: 0615848583
ISBN-13: 978-0615848587

SECOND EDITION

Originally published in 2003 by Xlibris.
The text of this edition contains all corrections and revisions that have been made since the original publication.

Design by Pepper Lillie.
www.pepperlillie.com

Silk Raven Press logo by Nichole Kohler

Deep Autumn is dedicated to:

Vince and Kathie Harrington,
the greatest parents a boy could ever wish for;

Ro-Ro, my grandmother and my first friend;

Kathie, my sister and my rock;

Margaux, mon frère and my first reader;

Cathie Gore, my soul mate;

and always,
this is for Dennis.

Deep Autumn is also dedicated to all the children who have suffered
abuse and learned to turn survival into triumph.

I would like to say thank you to:
Patti Smith
Uncle Jack Woods
Joyce Cronk
Vicky Lee & Craig McKelvey
Mike Yob

A special thank you to Beth Meier
for her assistance and enduring patience.

Here are some stories...

From *Webster's New Collegiate Dictionary* © 1975:

autumn

Noun

1: the season between summer and winter comprising, in the northern hemisphere, usually the months of September, October, and November or, as reckoned astronomically, extending from the September equinox to the December solstice—called also *fall*

2: a period of maturity or incipient decline <in the autumn of her life>

From *Years of Stepping on Dead Leaves* © 1967:

deep autumn

Noun

1: late October when all the clocks turn back time
2: the season of decay <the burning of the leaves>
3: a state of cyclical anxiousness <"caught in a trap / I can't walk out" (Elvis Presley)>
4: a last gasp <Indian summer>
5: suicidal ideation <can't see the driveway for the leaves>
6: visitation of past digressions occurring during periods of sleeplessness <the bone truth>
7: the time of the dares <a time to let go>

CONTENTS

Desire Stories

Stories Between

Stories of Abuse

Stories of Zen and Want

Redemption Stories

CONTENTS

"It's only fiction, mind you."
source unknown (controversy pending)

"Queenie, I never lost my hat."
Edward Joseph Woods, my grandfather

"Silence, exile, and cunning."
James Joyce, *A Portrait of the Artist as a Young Man*

Deep Autumn

Desire Stories

Sixty-Two in Eight

"I want you so it scares me to death."
Elvis Costello and the Attractions, "I Want You"

Recommended Soundtrack:

"I Want You" by Elvis Costello and the Attractions

"I've Been Loving You Too Long (To Stop Now)"
by Otis Redding

"Nightswimming" by R.E.M.

There she is with goddamn shaky Noel and a camera that costs a thousand dollars. Noel wasn't always shaky; that came later. When I first met him, he was top of the heap. Now he's shaky—big deal. I told her not to take any pictures, but does she listen? No. Sometimes life isn't art; sometimes it's just shit that happened or is happening right now and not all of it needs to be on black and white film from a camera that costs more than my car. I'm not sure what makes me crazier: goddamn shaky Noel or a camera that never stops clicking.

So now we're a foursome, and we're taking a walk to see where it happened. Winslet walks in front with Noel, and I'm next; Sandi is her divorced mom, and she follows me. Sandi told us where it was, and it seemed a better idea than sitting on the porch with nothing to do. But Winslet brings the camera, and my stomach isn't feeling so good; I know some things *need* to just be. If we were home, Noel would work on Winslet, and Sandi would take a nap, but I'm like the combustible element in this autumn equation: something *needed* to happen. "Let's take a walk, and I'll show you." That was Sandi. Winslet ran inside for the camera. "Okay," I said, but I knew it wasn't.

The first thing heard is "a little sightseeing?" and none of us say any words back, but Winslet looks as if she wants to. Winslet has no censor, see, and the first syllables that form when she opens her mouth are the ones that come out. "Shut the fucking door," she told me in the morning. I watch her carefully to be ready and cover with a joke because there's maybe nine of them and four of us, and we're out of our element.

They are playing cards outside, fanning themselves with *TV Guides*, and because their skin is black and ours isn't, we live in different worlds within the same neighborhood. The fire is theirs; it doesn't belong to us. Winslet is wearing the shortest cut-offs you ever did see and that camera around her neck. I say hi under my breath, and Noel asks Winslet if he can open her film or do anything for her. You can smell it from here although it's days old, maybe a week, and the people in the lawn chairs just stare and fan hot air, shaking their heads.

We cross the street and a boy goes by on a bicycle; he's probably six or seven. My stomach turns circles. We shouldn't be doing this. Sandi sucks on her lower lip and watches her toes wiggle in their sandals as we cross over. She's on the outside now; this thing between Noel and Winslet has to play itself out, but Sandi understands Noel will be gone soon, and I'm just the extra component. Sandi knows I wish she wasn't here, no offense. But Sandi likes me. I smile, and she stops biting her lip for a second. Sandi is alone and lives through Winslet, and Winslet lives through the camera lens. Maybe we all live through Winslet. None of us are happy, and maybe this is a way to see something worse so we know how good we have it—all that in a false smile.

"Tourists." We're across the road, but I hear them. I turn around, and a woman edges out of the screen door, speaking to the people splayed in lawn chairs. Her name is Brenda, but I don't know that yet. The yard is enclosed; two dogs yelp, and it's hard to hear. Somebody laughs. She is older, maybe forty, and her skin is like smooth paint. I watch her; she sees me, and now I lag behind. Brenda talks to the yard people, and there is another laugh. Her voice is like a wilted flower too long in the sun; maybe she's from the south. Walking here was like walking through the south—it's not like our side of the neighborhood—everyone was on a porch with a dog, and everyone said hi like it was the most natural thing in the world. They were the only real smiles I saw all day. But the people in the yard don't smile at all; the weight of the fire is theirs to bear.

Winslet dumped Noel some months back, but they are trying the friends thing on for size, and suddenly it's Labor Day weekend, and he's sleeping over. I know he's not having sex with her because I asked Winslet, and even though she was angry with me for asking, she told me no. "Friends sometimes sleep in other friends' beds," she said, but I've never slept in Winslet's bed. I don't bring that up though. I can't let on that I am chained to her love, because if I do I will disappear like smoke, and I have no one else in this world to talk to. A real dilemma, this, because I sometimes wish she were two people, so I wouldn't wonder if my small heart makes the friendship even smaller. This kind of thinking, Winslet tells me, will lead nowhere.

I also know someone else is trying to love Winslet. I know because on the walk over she uses a new word not once, not twice, but three times. "I believe everything is *impermanent*," she said when I told her she might be doing wrong by photographing the remains. I asked her where she found the word, and she revealed in whispers this someone new. It is his word, and Winslet is becoming that person—framing the new stranger in a certain way—letting him develop her. It is his word, but it's not Winslet's. The Winslet I know keeps journals with acid free paper and documents every new experience through a lens. I hope the new person hasn't gotten into her pants yet, but it can't be too far off if she's using his words.

And there they are: four twins, skeletons, a rubble driveway between each, set on a little skid of a road. The fire must have licked the bent tips of the single tree on the far corner. The boy on the bicycle is back, and he does a wheelie in the middle of the street. We're across from them, and my stomach does little flip-flops. "Sixty-two in eight," he says, and I cover my ears. Everything smells like a cigarette does when someone puts it out in a toilet. Sandi asks the little boy what he means by that, but she knows, we all know. Sixty-two in eight. The houses are charcoal rubbings, and the fence around the tiny front yard on the near corner, its once green wax melted clear down to the twisted metal, is covered with notes and flowers and stuffed animals.

The woman I will know soon as Brenda walks down the middle of the road with two small children. "Going to the store?" asks the boy on the bike, and he's off to beat her down the block. I stare as she passes. I want to ask if it's true, sixty-two in eight, but before I can she says to me, "Just a little boy playing with his mama's stove. That's his bear there." And I see it, fur peeled back to its marble eyes, tied to the fence with all the stuffed animals. Pinned to each of the ragged bears and worn dogs is a handwritten note in crayon— children's wishes. The other animals are from the fire department; they are shiny and don't belong here anymore than the four of us. The scorched bear is real like Brenda is real. I have to lean against a wall. The woman called Brenda reaches the corner and makes the turn. So much love stuck in such small houses, I think.

Winslet has the camera out, and she's focusing, and I scream at her, "You can't, you can't. It's sacred ground. Let it go." Winslet doesn't turn her head, but her shoulders rise, and she speaks into the camera. "If you don't want to be here, leave." And I say, "But it's sacred ground. It's not ours. You shouldn't take pictures. What's gone is gone." Sandi looks at me with the sorry eyes, and I realize for the first time what her eyes mean. "It's wrong," I say and walk up the block, the smell of burnt love strong in my nostrils. Sandi says something to Noel, but he's busy unwrapping film and holding Winslet's bags, whispering in her ear. Winslet says to her mother, so I can hear, "He's doing it on purpose."

My head is spinning; I keep walking so I don't throw up. Winslet promised we would go to the movies afterward, but I don't think we're going now; I get angry about that too. Winslet's camera goes *click click click*, stuttering echoes down the street. I want to turn and tell her again. I want to take all the cameras away from her face and kiss her until she surrenders to me, and her hair falls down my cheeks. *You can't capture what is sacred and you never ask me to sleep in your bed*: these are the things I want to tell her, but I just walk. I really don't want to let her out of my sight in case Noel tries to kiss her behind a tree, but I need to be far enough away so I can't hear the click of the camera or smell the scent of burnt teddy bear; I think I will always know both.

The boy on the bicycle skids to a stop and points to a white house with a side yard surrounded by a fence; a laundry line crosses from tree to tree. "That's where they chain the retarded boy when he wants to come out and play. We throw crabapples at him sometimes." And the tears come and clean the dirt off my face. "The pretty white girl's on one of the porches, you know." I close my eyes, and the boy on the bicycle rides away. I walk until I reach the iron shoulder of the road, woods on either side of the dead end, and sit my sorry ass down, crying until there's nothing left. Winslet says my heart is too small, and I have to love someone else. I have to let go too.

Sandi is there soon, and she says Winslet is finished and wants to maybe hike in the woods. I shake her off. Sandi says, "Let's go, Winslet wants to walk." I tell her I don't do everything Winslet wants like everyone else, and Sandi smiles. She knows I'm lying because my eyes cross when I do, and they are crossing like crazy. I am glad the sun is going down; in the dark, you can't see my eyes.

Winslet in her fashion shoes. Winslet with a camera that costs a thousand dollars. Winslet treading on sacred ground. Winslet spending her love again and again, moving from one Noel to another like she's trying to get love in focus. I'm too close, I think. I am too close to be in focus. I have nothing to offer but surrender.

My friends are gone, and I am alone on the side of the road. The only path I know home goes near the fire zone. I am afraid, but my feet take over, and I am walking before I know it. The undergrowth on either side of the road is thick, filling with night noises. One of those fuzzy little dandelion wishes floats toward me, and when I move out of its way, it circles back on the wind and follows me for damn near half a block.

I reach the house where Brenda lives. Only a few people are in the lawn chairs, and they are saying good-night to each other. Brenda is in the backyard with the milk she bought at the store, and she opens the gate for them as they leave. "Did you see my wish?" I ask her. She looks puzzled, holding the gate for me. I sit on a lawn chair. Brenda hands the milk to one of the little girls, and they run giggling around the back. It is so dark, and lightning bugs make little fires in the corners of my eyes. Brenda tells me her name. She is older than I am, and maybe the little girls are hers, and maybe they're not. Brenda takes my hand, and we walk into her house.

The living room is small, but I don't get a good look because Brenda leads me into a bedroom that is even smaller, filled to the ceiling with books and plants. I stand in the middle and try and count the number of ways this bedroom is different from Winslet's. I don't see any cameras, and suddenly everything is wet and bleary.

Brenda holds me close and asks if I'm crying about my wish. I spill my damn guts. I tell Brenda: "I'm guilty too. I want to capture everything that hurts and let go of nothing. I want to wear fashion shoes and own the right records. So much love in such a small heart. A beady little heart. Won't let go. Can't let go," but I know she doesn't understand a word. She smiles and asks me, "When was the last time you came?" I don't have an answer, but I feel what Brenda feels against her stomach, and I am ashamed.

"It's a favor. Friends do friends favors when they're down," she says, and when I sit on the bed, Brenda sits next to me. "He lived. He's in the hospital. I saw him the day before yesterday. He just wanted to play with his mama's stove, pretend he was a big person. His name is Roger. He'll have scars for a long time." Her hand is in my lap, and I tell her I should find Winslet in case something happens. Brenda kisses my temple. "Sometimes you just need to feel something real."

And when I wake up, the house is empty, but the street outside is noisy with kids. I drink the milk Brenda bought at the store and sit outside, fanning myself with a *TV Guide*. Brenda comes around the corner and holds my hand. "Nothing stays around forever; you need to be still while everything changes just to catch your breath," Brenda says. I want to tell her I'm tired of being still, but I don't dare.

"Looks like rain; could have used it last week," she says, and I nod and wait for water to come down from the sky.

-end-

Wallpaper Notes

"Oh, since the day I saw you / I have been waiting for you
You know I will adore you / 'Til eternity."
The Ronettes, "Be My Baby"

Recommended Soundtrack:

"Be My Baby" by the Ronettes

"Where Has Our Love Gone?"
by Diana Ross and the Supremes

"Bathysphere"
{live bootleg version, Washington DC 9-18-96}
by Cat Power

I wasn't crying, she says, *my eyes were. I am disconnected from my body.* The man points to her tears, but she corrects him, corrects him twice. *My eyes were*, she says. He asks: *am I hurting you?* And she says: *only as much as I need*, and he looks at her funny. At least she thinks he does. Her eyes are still swimming; it is hard to tell.

I want you to feel good too, he says. She does not believe him; his tone is automated like when she tries to call her dad and his number's been changed. *Please check the number and try your call again.* She loved him above all men—her father, that is. The man on top of her has white hair like her dad's but more than her dad ever did, or at least more than she remembers him having. The man also has little white tufts sprouting from his fleshy back and a white trail that curves up and down, up and down his great big ball of a stomach, ending down there where all things must end. This man is not at all like her father; this man smells of bars and Pall-Malls and fear. Her father smelled of rough soap and cut grass.

creak creak

Her head is pinned beneath the man's flaccid arms, soaked with sweat, but she manages a glimpse toward the window: no proper shade there, just paper hung askew. She needs one more thumbtack, just one more, and the paper shade would hang balanced. As it is, a sliver of light (sunlight, streetlight, moonlight, she isn't sure) peeks through. One more thumbtack—but why buy a whole box when she needs only one? That's her philosophy in a nutshell: don't take more than you need.

She tilts her head again to study the streak of light, to determine its origin, its portents. She often contemplates the hidden meanings of the mundane while working; she calls these Reoccurring Thoughts. They are mulled over again at bedtime when she rubs her toes against the bottom lining of her blanket ten times before resigning herself to sleep. *Everything has a place and the world has a place for everything*, her father told her once. Is the streak of light a sign of what is to come or a symbol of how little light there is left in the world?

creak creak creak

The man makes a sound and moves faster: *quick stroke quick stroke quick stroke*. She feels his balls; they are tight. He is ready, and she has already forgotten his name. Maybe he doesn't have a name. She never needed one, not since the ice show. *Baby* was good enough for her father, and it seems just enough for the men who climb the dark stairway and spend time in the room with no proper shade, just paper hung askew. *Baby baby baby where did our love go?* Her father would sing, and they would forget Mom had left with someone her dad had once called a friend. *Please hang up and try the number again.*

creak creak creak creak

The man moans *baby*, and she supposes she should feel him shooting up inside of her secret place, but she feels nothing. It is Not Her, she determines. *I wasn't crying*, she said, *my eyes were*—and truer words were never spoken. It is Not Her, and he is finished (for now); he makes little grunting noises as he pushes himself off the bed—stumbles—runs his hand down where she is sure little white whiskers occasionally gather.

"You want a drink?"

She answers him, *no thank you*, she isn't very thirsty, *but thank you.* Not Her would have to take a shower soon before his stuff dries inside her like a prune and sticks. Not Her should have held fast to the rubber rule, but the Trojan split in two even though his thing was small, and she is out of rubbers like she is out of thumbtacks.

The long thin triangle of light makes the room appear larger, makes the room look like Patrick's. All the rooms in Patrick's house were bigger than hers and her dad's. She squints at the window. Nighttime, she guesses, and it's raining; the cars all sound funny, like they have little rockets under them. That's how you know it's raining, she thinks. *God's way of crying*, her father would say. It's raining cats and dogs like when Patrick stayed over that last night, and they counted the cars outside, trying to guess if it was a truck or a station wagon or a sports car by the sounds of the rockets beneath the tires.

silence

The man lurches back into the room and speaks to Not Her like he is talking to a puppy. Not Her tries to focus on his mouth, but all she can see are the places where his teeth should have been—and then she remembers knocking out Patrick's tooth in the fifth grade.

Patrick Patrick Patrick. She knocked it clear out, and he said it was okay, and he called her the nickname he always called her when they were alone. She had been swinging on the tire for an hour, waiting, and had tied her hair in two ponytails, and even though it wasn't blonde, it could have passed, for it was summertime. She was waiting for Patrick because he was her only friend (besides her dad), and he never said her mom left because she was a whore and the whole town knew it, knew it by heart. The tire swing went higher and higher, and she never heard him sneak up from behind the old tree.

When he threw the chocolate bar into her lap, she spun around mid-swing *(shazam)* and kicked out his tooth. He was always bringing her treats from his big house; they would share the tire swing, gobble the treats, listen to the branch go *creak creak* like a clock going *tick tock* as they swayed back and forth in the summer wind.

silence

The man is telling Not Her about his ex-wife or third wife or some wife. Not Her nods in time to the beat of his words. She never understands why they talk—*talk like a woman,* her father would have said. Once they leave the seed, if there's still time, they always talk. She likes it better when they don't look at her face, even when they are inside of her and especially after they are done. Another Reoccurring Thought: why do they keep talking about the bad things that brought them here when they just rid themselves of the worst? She needn't worry about it now; Not Her has it under control and even responds with an *awww* at the man's downhearted face.

Patrick didn't look downhearted when she kicked out his tooth; Patrick didn't even cry. He sat on the ground and held his face for a long time. She stayed on the tire and watched him like he was at the end of a telescope; she hoped she hadn't done it on purpose because Patrick was her only friend and never called her mother a whore. But sometimes she did things called acting out by the nuns—and she shouldn't do these things because *you don't want to end up like your mother, do you?* Her dad had to come to school when she acted out—when she had used the boys' room to pee because the line was too long for the girls', and the other time when she had carved a picture of a butterfly on her desk with a Swiss Army Knife. When the principal (who was also a nun) said *you don't want her to end up like, well, like, you know,* her dad told the nun she better hope the Lord didn't hear her talk such trash, because the Lord has a built-in lie detector, and she was so full of shit her eyes were brown. Daddy never punished his Baby when he picked her up at the school office; instead, he would cook spaghetti rather than order out, and they would dance and dance and dance while they waited for the water to boil.

She hoped she wasn't acting out now and said so aloud to Patrick. Then she started to laugh, because it was funny not to know if you were acting out or not, and Patrick stood up and started to walk away; she saw how little he was (seven months younger, after all), and her laugh caught in her throat, and her eyes were two quarters at the bottom of a fountain. Both of them crawled around for a little while on their hands and knees until they found the tooth. Patrick said a fairy would bring him money for it, and he would split it with her fifty-fifty since she kind of did all the work. She felt the quarters slip deeper into the fountain, and Patrick said it was okay, *don't cry*, because they would be married someday, *and what's a tooth between married people!* And then Patrick called her the nickname he always called her when they were alone.

silence

The man is stroking Not Her's thigh, and his voice is hoarse, his breathing laborious. She hopes he doesn't touch himself. She hates when they do that because the veins on their necks bulge out, and they look like her father the time he stood in the doorway amid the steam from her clothes all wet with rain across the radiator, the steam crawling up to hide her father's eyes. She wishes the man would just climb on top and do it (again!) and leave. *I want you to feel good too*, he repeats, and Not Her smiles like the cat that ate the canary. It is Not Her's job to make their veins bulge—and not look away. Not Her could stay here all night (if it really is night) and talk to the men (if more are coming over, that is; she can't remember) who climb the dark stairway to spend time and talk and seed.

Patrick Patrick Patrick. Because she was older, she taught him card tricks and showed him how to dance to the *baby baby baby where did our love go?* Patrick defended her in school when they called her the whore's daughter and when they asked her if she thought maybe the man who brought the mail was her real father. Patrick told her about the butterfly's view and taught her to *float float float*. He tried to kiss her just about every other day, and she would giggle and say to him: *float float* just *float*. She figured she would kiss him all the time someday, so she held out for just the right moment, and even her father joked and called them: *two peas in a pod*. Her father said he didn't much care for Patrick because he had money and therefore wouldn't think twice about hurting a girl who didn't have a pot to piss in, but her dad was never mean. When Patrick's father left home, and his mother mounted martinis all the day long, her dad said *pain and suffering doesn't know from money*, and he let Patrick stay over and sleep on a cot in the hallway near her room. Her father would ask: *How's it feel on the other side of the tracks, Patrick?* Patrick liked her house even though the dishes didn't match and the rooms were small and her mother had left because she was a whore.

silence

The man turns Not Her on her stomach and is mumbling into her ear. She moves her head so she can see the shadow patterns the rain makes on the wall, the droplets caught red-handed in the streak of light. Yes, she had heard the rumors, she told her dad, rumors of Patrick's father and her mother. *This isn't the first time Patrick's father left home for a spell, you understand,* and she understood and felt a little flutter in her stomach for Patrick, a little flutter of a wing uncovering something deep and dark and hidden. She wanted to help Patrick float. If her father was the one warm mass in her life, a blanket to cover her toes when it was cold, Patrick was her touchstone, the person who brought her back to earth and fed her chocolate bars when the other kids would kick at her heels and call her a whore's daughter, daughter of a whore, and the whole town knows it, knows it by heart.

creak creak creak creak creak

Not Her is on all fours trying not to hit her head on the stained wallpaper, the wallpaper that peels conveniently when she has to leave herself a note. She did that yesterday—tore off a piece and scribbled down two words, but she forgets where she hid it and can't remember what she wrote. *Does that feel good?* The man with the great big ball of a stomach asks: *do you like it, do you like it, does it feel good?* (Float float float.) Not Her answers him, and he goes back to making soft little pig noises in her ear. She felt something down there once, down there in the secret place. Her father told her: *everything has a place and the world has a place for everything.* She assumes her secret place has been around the world a few times, so to speak, but only once did she actually feel anything stir—only once, and it was sweet, oh so sweet.

Once in the rain, you were calling my name: Patrick singing to her, and both of them running because the autumn drops were like old Hershey's Kisses, and she said to Patrick: *I never thought rain could really hurt!* And Patrick said: *I guess everything hurts if you get too much, but never you mind that.* They ran to her house (her father wasn't home from work), and they undressed with their backs turned, placing their wet clothes across the radiator. She gave him old pajamas to wear, the kind with feet. She donned a similar pair, and they found they could slide across the kitchen tiles like two ice skaters. *Be careful of the crack on the floor.* That was Patrick, always looking out for the traps, the foibles he called them. Steam was rising from the radiator, and

Patrick said it was smoke for their ice show. *Baby baby baby where did our love go? Of course he'll let you stay, it's hailing taxis and dogs out there.* They giggled and skated and twirled. *I got this yearning burning yearning feeling inside me*; she tried to sing and dance like the Supremes her father had shown her on the television. Her pajama feet snagged on the broken tile, and her head hit the stove before she fell because the kitchen was so small.

Patrick rubbed her noggin and offered his sleeve (her eyes were leaking) and said: *I told you to float, not fly.* And they both laughed, and she felt warm in his arms, and she kissed him on his soft little lips, upturned like butterfly wings mid-flight. He looked different to her, or maybe she just noticed how beautiful he was for the first time: his skin smooth and slightly darker than hers, with little hairs soft like down in a good pillow, and the hair on his head, awkward and black, sticking up in places like a cartoon character's. He touched his fingers to her lips; she held her hand over his face. *Patrick Patrick Patrick.* She kissed him again and decided he tasted like chocolate.

creak creak creak creak creak creak

Not Her is now flat on her stomach, and the man's belly goes *flap flap flap* against her back, his veiny nose buried in her hair that is not blonde, her hair that is no longer tied in ponytails. The man gulps air *oh baby*, heaving his white tuft covered body onto hers *oh baby*, and Not Her takes it without blinking. *Baby baby baby.* She smells his cologne and something musty and old and medicinal all at the same time; it is almost enough to make even Not Her gag and bite into a pillow. She concentrates on the sliver of light, dusty as if from a movie projector.

She led Patrick to her bed and stretched down next to him. They counted the cars outside—tried to guess if it was a truck or a station wagon or a sports car by the sounds of the rockets beneath the tires. *Once in the rain, you were calling my name.* She took his warm hand and placed it down her pajama bottoms. Baby closed her eyes: she was on the tire swing, higher and higher, and could almost taste the clouds in the back of her mouth. She opened her eyes, and now the steam was a cloud and Patrick's eyes two moons, two moist glowing moons. He went to say something, and she brushed her hand across the stiffness poking his pajama bottoms, just lightly brushed the outside, and he stopped talking. She closed her eyes again (higher and higher) and swallowed the clouds, felt Patrick's soft hand under her pajamas, beneath her underwear, all the way inside her, and Patrick's breathing:

short, hard, steady. Patrick's hand was inside, and they were two peas in a pod, and no one could pull asunder what has been brought together here today. No. One. Could. Pull. Asunder. What. Has. Been. Brought. Together. Here. Today.

The bedsprings went *creak creak* like the branch that held the tire swing, like a clock going *tick tock*.

She opened her eyes: her father was in the doorway, blocking the light from the kitchen.

"Daddy?"

His face shifted and changed in the steam from the radiator, and his eyes were two headlights boring down on her, and *Patrick Patrick Patrick* was across the room, a heap at the bottom of a wall. Glass tinkled, and someone screamed, and her mouth filled with blood, and her lower lip hung from her face like a dead butterfly's wing. *Shazam.* Her father was gone—back to the bar from where he never returned, and, oh, Patrick, sweet Patrick, he was gone too. She used her secret place for money and rode a bus and cursed each red light and, oh, sweet Patrick. They picked him off the floor like a limp doll, and her father—they found her father at the bar, and they took him in and locked him away and swallowed the key and oh, Patrick, sweet Patrick, where has our love gone?

creak creak creak creak creak creak creak

Not Her's arms are pinned, and the man pounds until her back and rear are numb. She can't feel when he finishes. His lips press against her neck, and Not Her can smell the bar and the Pall-Malls and the fear. *Jesus, sweet Jesus*, the man says to himself as he gets to his feet.

Her voice creases the night: "Chocolate bar!"

"What?"

Not Her is gone—back inside to lick her wounds and prepare for the next rendezvous. She remembers the note torn from the wall: just two words. She tries to rise from the bed and finds her legs numb; she beats her calves with fists and gouges her thighs with broken nails until pins and needles go *creak creak creak* like a clock goes *tick tock tick tock tick tock*. The man stares and whistles *sweet Jesus*. She pulls herself off the bed and makes it halfway to the door—falls—the faded yellow sheet twisted around blotched legs.

"Ain't you a sight?"

Oh Patrick, sweet Patrick!

"Get up!"

Daddy, it was so sweet, so sweet.
"Cryin' for no good reason…blatherin' away…"
I wasn't crying, she says, *my eyes were. I am disconnected from my body.*

-end-

endgame

"And then I see a darkness
Did you know how much I love you?"
Johnny Cash, "I See a Darkness"

Recommended Soundtrack:

"I See A Darkness" by Johnny Cash

"Highway Kind" by Townes Van Zandt

"I'm Not In Love" by Tori Amos

i could smell the rain
in puddles around your feet,
descending your arches,
tracing the long bone now slick,
like the lies we feed ourselves

"…thief…"

the rain was almost perfect,
a laugh caught midstream;
i could see your face in the puddle,
in the puddle i could make out your face;
and the shadow behind you,
and the shadow behind you was mine

"…ruiner…"

the splash took no time at all
but consumed it
like lies in puddles around my feet

Stories Between

An Open-Ended Wish

"These rivers of suggestion are driving me away."
R.E.M., "So. Central Rain (I'm Sorry)"

Recommended Soundtrack:

"So. Central Rain (I'm Sorry)" by R.E.M.

"I Want A Little Sugar In My Bowl" by Nina Simone

"Crazy" by Patsy Cline

"Swingin' Party" by the Replacements

ngel had outlasted almost all of them and was helping Michael and her cousin Jessie drag the turntable out from underneath the basement stairs. Most of the revelers had long since given up the ghost and either left for home or found a nook or cranny in which to hang their heads. Angel's brother Peter lived in the basement, and the acquisition of the turntable had resulted in the partial awakening of one of Peter's more comatose friends, who had curled into a ball halfway under the stairs; a hand reached out and began caressing Jessie's ankle.

"I left the present on the bed, baby."

"What did he say?"

"He's touching my ankle."

"Did he give you a present, Jess?"

"No, but I think he'd like to. Can we hurry this up?"

Michael had drunk too much and feared he would slur his speech. He said nothing but reached down and removed the offender's hand from Jessie's ankle.

"Thanks, Michael."

He nodded in the dark, and as Jessie turned to help Angel lift the Emerson, he could smell faint traces of bath oil beneath the gin and cigarette ambiance of Tabbi's seventh annual.

"I tied it off with a bow, baby."

"Shouldn't he be out cold? Can we just hurry up?"

"Why are we getting this thing again, Jess?"

+

The Nina Simone record was badly scratched, and the cover was replete with the outline of the vinyl within. It looked to Michael like a watermark on a bar; the music inside left watermarks too. He had bought it from the used book and record shop where he worked and had agonized over the selection, passing Aretha, Townes, Leonard, and even Tom Waits in his search. Michael had counted on, among other things, Angel or her mother Tabbi having a functioning turntable.

"Can we unplug this, Angel?"

"You can unplug whatever you want, boy. I'm out of here. Kiss me, fools."

"Thanks for inviting me, Angel."

"Yeah, yeah."

Angel kissed her cousin good-night and disappeared around the corner.

"Are you going to tell me why the turntable, Mike?"

"Michael. Well, I bought you a Christmas present. It's nothing really."

Jessie laughed, and Michael memorized every line on her face.

"Let me guess! It's a record."

Michael handed her Nina Simone. He freshened a gin and tonic while she perused the liner notes.

"I don't know her."

"Oh, well, she's terrific, really."

Small talk was not his forte, but then again, the only thing he felt completely comfortable with was writing. But that was for later; now he wanted to let the gin do its job and let Jessie glimpse the normally reticent Michael. He hoped Angel wouldn't eavesdrop on them; it was an old house, and even with the wind kicking like it was, he could clearly hear the splatters of someone running a shower on the second floor. He planned to kiss Jessie before the long ride home— unless, of course, she asked him to stay.

+

Angel let her mind go to pieces like the drops of water breaking upon the stiffness of her back. She had touched the new boy's hand tonight and had kissed him—on his ear. The boy has been in her mother's employment only four weeks; before today she had only glimpsed him and his shyness in her mom's office. She didn't think him beautiful; Angel had become obsessed by the bump on his nose. Inviting the new boy to the party was a mistake.

Hands on hands on hands on hands. Angel had pretended to whisper good-night and kissed his ear instead. She brought her water-wrinkled fingers to her lips. *Hands on hands on hands on lips.* She had shared a footstool-turned-chair with him and had leaned forward to reach her lip balm, almost brushing his hard-on with her arm. Angel felt a sudden urge for sugar; sugar and sex just seemed to go together. She thought: *hands on hands on hands on you-know-what*, and turned the cold water down. The warmth felt good on her back; she wrote the new boy's name on the shower door. And there again—Angel trapped him in the backdoor of her mind:

"Shhh. You don't want anyone to hear us do you?"

He shakes his head.
"Do you want me to stop?"
He looks down.
"Why are you getting up? You can sleep here like everyone else."
He tries to wriggle under her arms. He nods his head.
"You don't want to wake anyone, do you?"
He stops moving; he stops nodding his head.

Angel turned the cold water completely off and let her back scald for a second before leaping out. She wiped his name off with her arm. The new boy had been rubbing her arms when Jon had walked in from the kitchen. Angel hadn't expected him for a few hours more; Jon was going to party with his friends before coming to her mother's.

She towel dried her hair violently. Jon was wearing that face when he walked into the living room and then hid it beneath his toothy smile. Angel knew the look, and as she left the new boy and embraced her boyfriend, she cursed the familiarity. The new boy disappeared shortly after Jon's entrance. Now Jon was sleeping the party off in her bedroom while she was dreaming of the bump on the new boy's nose and writing his name on the shower door. Jon put up with her shit, and she almost loved him for it.

Angel looked at herself in the mirror; she could barely see her face through the steam. Would she look different if the new boy's gestures were as ingrained in her as Jon's? Did the new boy look at her and see the same eyelashes and lips and laugh lines as Jon? *Hands on hands on hands on lies.* Angel sat on the lid of the toilet, slumped forward, her eyes peering out from beneath wet strands. Nina Simone drifted from the vent. She would be consumed by the new boy if she let herself. Angel wondered, not for the first time, if each new boy helped define her or merely chipped away at something precious.

+

Jessie had placed the vinyl on the Emerson turntable, and Nina was tumbling out like single malt over hand chopped ice. Michael was studying a photograph of Angel and Jessie in faux 1920's outfits. Angel was a photographer, and Michael admired her work and, even more so, admired the distant and estranged look captured in Jessie's eyes: here was a woman not content with her station; here was a woman for whom the next train was less an adventure than an escape route from her soul's most recent passage. It didn't hurt that the photograph was extremely flattering to Jessie's muscular thighs.

Nina lamented the loss of her man. Michael touched the folded squares in his back pocket.

"Do you like the photograph?"

"Yes. I mean, Angel's great. Her work just breathes, you know..."

Jessie flashed a grin, and Michael blushed.

"I like it."

"Do you think my breasts look bigger in that picture?"

"Your what?"

"My breasts. Well, not bigger exactly, but more attentive, as if Angel had a crew holding them up."

Michael resisted a comparison study.

"Do you like Nina?"

Jessie twirled about the room and came to rest on the coffee table.

"Sit next to me. What the hell is in your back pocket?"

Michael sat on the edge of the coffee table.

"It's a story I wrote for you."

"For me? Hmm. Tell me, does this approach work often for writers?"

"I'm sorry?"

"Nothing. Let me see."

"No, first you have to play the wish game with me."

"The wish game? Okay, I'm game. Pour me another glass of the red, will you?"

+

Michael brought the glass over with two pencils and two sheets of paper.

"It's not a game, really. You write down three wishes for the New Year, and I write down three wishes too. It's usually a drinking thing. If you guess the other person's wishes, they have to drink. If any of our wishes are close or the same, well, it's just good luck then."

"I don't know about drinking much more, but I'll play."

Michael wrote down the same wish three times and folded the paper over. Jessie took more time, and laughed quietly to herself.

Nina demanded the presence of some sugar in her bowl.

"I like this song. Which one is this?"

Jessie leaned toward the phonograph. Michael's hand touched hers for a second.

" 'Sugar in My Bowl.' Will you dance with me?"

Michael put one hand on her waist and found the other between her soft fingers.

"Why is your heart beating so?"

Jessie swung her head back and smiled to the ceiling, their hands crushed together behind her back.

"You really want to kiss me right now, don't you, Michael?"

Her tongue tasted like wine and her lips like raw berries in late winter. He wanted to kiss the soft slope of her shoulder. He hoped she couldn't feel his hard-on.

+

Angel dressed herself for bed in the dark. She could hear husky breathing from Jon asleep and awash in booze across the room, bundled beneath her blankets. *Oh, to release myself from this mess*, she thought, the words descending like an old blues song. *The bump on his nose, the bump on his nose*—Angel didn't need to drink to feel this. Jon turned in his sleep. There he was: a pal, an old dog—Angel even knew what he smelled like after a long night's sleep. She knew nothing of the new boy's scents and wondered how she smelled to him inhaled through his nose with the intoxicating bump.

From across the hall, her mother hummed Patsy Cline and shuffled her way down the stairs, her slippers keeping time.

Angel stuck her head out of her bedroom door.

"Where's Alvin?"

Her mother turned, lost her step, and one slipper descended the stairs alone.

"Alan. His name is Alan."

"Where is he?"

"Home, I guess. I sent him home."

"Why?"

Tabbi shrugged.

"It was time. Time's up!"

"Good-night."

"Good-night."

Angel closed the door and leaned against it, her skin still pulsing warm from the shower. Angel thought her mother bloodless. Not cold blooded. Quite monogamous (usually). Not loose. Just bloodless. Her mother's life was a flipbook of lovers and suitors and proposals and the occasional drunken grasps in parked cars. A man would appear, eat dinner with the family, go to the movies, put his feet on the coffee table, shake her father's hand at family functions requiring the presence of both parental units—then, poof, the man would be gone, banished, a blur in the rearview mirror. Bloodless. Next adventure. For a woman of fifty, her mother looked ten years younger, and her abandon required her fluids to reach a boiling point—if the temperature dropped, so did the significant other.

Sasha, Angel's oldest cat, rubbed against her leg, and then walked into the bureau; Sasha's eyes had burned to slight embers some years ago. Time was oh-so not on her side either, Angel thought. It was autumn when Angel first realized her mind unraveled during sex with Jon. It was in October, the sneakiest of months, when she found herself imagining a stranger pinning down her arms and gnawing away at her boredom. But time slipped away until the lump in a bed became a fiancée, became a permanent fixture. No hands on hands on hands. No bumps on noses. Angel knew her New Year's wish: she wanted to be just like her mother.

+

"You kids and that crazy music. Oh, hi."

The last word was drawn out for effect. Tabbi stood in the dining room clad in a long t-shirt.

"Aunt Tabbi has the greatest legs, doesn't she?"

"Hi, Tabbi. Did the music wake you?"

"No, no. I'm just so wired I figured a glass of wine might slow me down. But I can see that I entered mid-story, so I'll just grab a glass and go."

"You weren't interrupting anything, Aunt Tabbi."

Michael slumped in a chair, and the needle skipped a beat.

"No, no. I'm gone. You have a good night, kids."

+

Tabbi leaned against the old rolltop desk in the hall for balance.

The wine was kicking awake the swimming ounces upon ounces of alcohol already in her bloodstream. Angel's door was closed, her son and his friends were passed out in the basement, and her niece was making out with Michael from the old neighborhood. Absently, Tabbi ran her hands over the desk cover like she was strumming a guitar. Most people would use the desk to organize, to sort and pay bills. Tabbi paid her bills sprawled in bed amid her and Angel's seven cats.

What the rolltop desk contained were letters—stacks of letters and notes and little cards that arrived with bouquets of flowers. Tabbi thought: *a history in the making, if you will*. Buried beneath yellowed envelopes was the farewell note from her first love before he shipped out to Vietnam. On top of those were lined stationary with careful loops from the man who became her husband when the first boy never came home, the man to whom she maintained a congenial relationship even after the divorce. There, the fun began. Correspondence with a tale to tell: Joseph, Victor, Tom, the other Tom, Anthony—and somewhere, sunk deep within the heart of the desk, a wax-sealed love letter with a seal she had never dared to break. Tabbi laughed to herself thinking of how the rolltop desk would open in the next day or two and how the deposit of the newly departed Alan's letters might finally tip the balance and crash the old heap down to the next floor. Tabbi climbed between the blankets, laden with cats, humming "Crazy," her dressmaker's dummy, seldom used, standing watch over the empty side of the bed.

+

Jessie kneeled down on the floor and leaned her head in Michael's lap.

"I should go to bed too. I have to be getting back tomorrow. Long drive."

Michael remembered what Angel had told him earlier that night of Jessie's current relationship, of her tepid boyfriend and his country music cheating ways, and how Angel had held Michael up as a gentleman. He decided one kiss was all he needed to leave with tonight.

"Can I take you out sometime, Jessica?"

Zeus, one of Angel's cats, bounced into his lap. Michael managed to remain perfectly still while Jessie stroked the cat's fur. Zeus soon sashayed out of sight into the dining room. If he touched a cat, his hands would expand to the size of balloons. Nina was finishing a minor-key number. Michael knew it was the last song on that side.

"I'm sorry, Michael. What did you say?"

"I asked what your New Year's wishes were?"

"Oh, well, I didn't have any. Not yet. I have a few resolutions, but not too many wishes. I just drew a picture of a flying dragon on the paper instead. Sorry."

Jessie stood up and stretched. Michael pretended to look at a magazine cover.

"I'm going up now, okay? Are you all right to drive?"

"Peachy keen, Josephine."

Michael pulled the story out his back pocket and unfolded it.

"Don't forget this."

Jessie took the papers, and their fingers fumbled around each other's.

"Sorry."

"What's the story called?"

" 'An Open-Ended Wish.' "

"Clever."

"I try."

Jessie leaned down and kissed his forehead

"Happy New Year, Michael."

"Same—same to you."

+

Angel could feel Jon watching her; his breathing gave him away. Her eyes faced the ceiling, and the guilt she tried to purge in the shower creepy-crawled over her goose bumps. *Eyes on eyes on eyes on flesh.* Jon didn't pretend to roll over in his sleep, pushing silent suggestions with an erection hammering against her side. He just stared and measured his breathing to mimic sleep. Angel knew if she turned over, they would have the first sex of the New Year. *Hands on hands on hands on flesh.* She too could pretend, she thought, and as she turned to face Jon, Angel closed her eyes until the little streaks of light behind her eyelids washed over her like baptismal fireworks, and as Jon entered, she felt his face for a bump on his nose.

+

Maybe she'd dismissed Alan too soon. Tabbi moaned into her pillow, and her fingers clutched at the frayed edge of the mattress. The cats abandoned the bed as her legs clenched themselves into her stomach.

Crazy…crazy for feeling so lonely.

When the bed commenced spinning in opposite rotation to the ceiling, Tabbi felt her very blood might explode across the sheets and paint the walls, exposing every failure, every cheap motel, every expensive suite, the infidelities, the bumps in the night. Tabbi concentrated on the dressmaker's dummy standing guard at the side of her bed.

Save me save me save me!

Still the room traversed in circles. *Crazy for feeling so blue.* Tabbi cried out again to the dressmaker's dummy, called to her guardian angel, her voice whisper-hoarse, her eyes dried crimson.

Save me save me Jesus fucking Christ save me!

The only answer: a soft murmuring from Angel's room.

Tabbi pushed the sheets away and stumbled into the bathroom. Floating up from the downstairs, she could hear Michael taking his leave from Jessie over the sounds of her own sickness. Back in the hallway, Tabbi shoved the rolltop cover open and, in the dark, let her hands travel over the hills and valleys until her fingers found the wax seal. *Where are you now?* Rubbing its intricate pattern, Tabbi mouthed the sender's name over and over until she felt she could no longer stand, until his name became one again with her bloodstream. *Do you remember the kiss?* Downstairs, the back door slammed. *Who do you love?* Tabbi traced her fingers off the seal and bunched a small pile of letters in her hand. The dressmaker's dummy was not enough. She curled beneath her covers and littered the bed with love letters, burying her body in their words and exhortations and promises made in the dark until she passed out in the coming light of the New Year.

+

Michael sat in the dark for a while before deciding to leave. He turned Nina over and left side two playing as he exited from the kitchen door, pausing to pet one of the cats on his way out. Once outside, he reached into his pocket, and with a piece of scotch tape from the album's wrapping paper, hung his single wish, written three times, on the back door. Old snow crunched under his shoes as he made his way to his car. For a moment, Michael considered making a snow angel but thought better of it. In the car, he struggled to find a song he could identify with on the radio, and failed. He concentrated on the *wish-wish* of the windshield wipers as new snow was preparing to cover the old.

-end-

"Billy, We Gotta Get Outta Here"

"I got stones in my passway
and my road seems dark as night."
Robert Johnson, "Stones in My Passway"

Recommended Soundtrack:

"Stones In My Passway" by Robert Johnson

"I Can't Stand It Anymore" by the Velvet Underground

"Town Without Pity" by the Brian Setzer Orchestra

The first time was in autumn; it is winter now.

"Billy, we gotta get outta here."

It has been snowing for the past three days, and the plows have yet to reach the parking lot three floors below. Billy yawns. The office they both work in is closed, and the air in the room is thick from intermittent heat blasts. Star charts are strewn about the floor. They are in the Hub Motel.

The letter is on the nightstand. It is 11:15 AM.

She whispers:

"Goddamn, the parking lot is filled with empty beer cans. I never saw so many empty beer cans, I swear. Billy, come look at this. They're poking out of the snow."

Billy covers his eyes and peers at Tina through his fingers. Tina works nights at a beauty salon; she switches hair color more often than Billy changes his underwear. Her dyed red hair pushes against the windowpane; he can hear the crinkle of hair spray against the glass. Billy wouldn't be surprised to see stiff chunks of red fall at her feet.

He leans back against two pillows to solidify his position, legs still tucked beneath the worn blanket; his free hand plays over the nubbies. The blanket is so thin, Billy thinks, the only way to keep warm is to keep fucking, and if he keeps fucking Tina, they will never leave this room. He isn't sure how feels about that.

"Billy, we gotta get outta this place."

Tina walks around to what would only be referred to as her side of the bed if the room were in an apartment or a house with a little side garden. She wears a long white t-shirt over the muscular path her shoulders cut through the dyed red forest. The outline of her stomach is visible just below the name of the concert venue. Billy notes that while he can see her belly, her breasts are not visible beneath the nightshirt.

She lights a cigarette, Marlboro 100, and climbs next to him, her thighs a creamy contrast to the yellow blanket. Thick, her thighs are thick, Billy thinks. Not fat, thick. Not much cellulite either—a big boned girl. He likes it when girls have just a slight overabundance of flesh, like baby fat on their legs or a slight bulge just below their belly button. "We worship the flaws," he whispers to himself. Looking at her legs, he feels himself grow excited beneath the blanket. Ignore the belly, he muses, and you're home free. Ignore the belly that has outgrown its cute baby fat and was becoming insect-like and scaly, and maybe you can be between those legs for a record fourth time today. Hell, it isn't even noon.

Tina catches his eye and turns her back toward him, her butt against his arm. He can see a large yellow bruise on the back of her left leg. Did he do that?

"We can't stay here forever, Billy. We probably have to work tomorrow, you know."

He can smell cigarette smoke mixed with old body wash. Neither of them showered this morning. Billy rubs her thigh and wonders if she would fuck him in the shower.

"Why do we always come here? I mean, if we're going to be together every weekend, why don't we just get a little place. No, stop it, I mean it. I know you don't like Stacy, so we don't go over there, but I feel like I'm paying rent on an apartment that I'm not ever at."

Billy winces. His hands are working like an eraser over the yellow bruise. Don't pay attention to anything she says, or you'll never get it up, he thinks.

"We could get a little place, you know, that doesn't have beat up curtains and shit in the bottom of the bathtub."

She turns her head toward his and blinks at his face. Her lower lip curls into her teeth.

"We could get two bedrooms. We could put all my hair stuff in one for practice and your guitar too."

His hands are not removing the yellow bruise. Billy stops rubbing and takes a closer look. No, it wouldn't be where he would have grabbed her during some rough foreplay. He places his thumb over the bruise. No, bigger than his thumb. Fucking thing looks like Australia. Maybe Alaska.

"Are you even listening to me? Billy, we have to make a move here."

Her ass wobbles, and the two-pound ashtray near the foot of the bed shifts slightly.

"Off me, Billy. I'm talking here, okay? I'm trying to talk to you."

Definitely Australia. Did he see it last night? How about Friday night? When they left the bar, he tried to take her in the parking lot, but he had to piss and couldn't concentrate. They immersed themselves in each other throughout the night when they arrived here. Did he bruise her when he pushed her against the car or later when he took her from behind?

The letter is sealed and addressed and waiting on the nightstand. It is 11:48 AM.

"Stacy says that she can tell I'm happy just by the look on my face. You know how some people can just tell, just like that? Well, she's one of them. Every time a customer comes in and something's not right, Stacy knows as soon as they sit in her chair. Bang. Just like that. It's in the stars, Billy. Just look at our signs. You can't change destiny. You can't."

Who was she with before him? Has she been with someone else? That is *not* his bruise, he is sure. Is she sleeping with someone else? An image of Marti skates through his mind. Marti is in somebody else's bed, and the thought makes him sick to his stomach. Has Tina been in somebody else's bed?

"Are you even fucking listening to me?"

She stubs the Marlboro out. The brown glass ashtray threatens to jump when she turns to face him.

"How did you get that bruise on your leg?"

"Sink." She lights another. "At work."

"You just put one out," he says.

"We need to talk, Billy. We can't stay here. We have to go."

She reaches down between his legs, over the blanket.

"Billy…"

He looks at the television; the sound is off. A woman in a bright yellow suit is talking through a tight grin; the makeup around her mouth looks hastily applied—as if she hasn't removed years and years of layers. Marti used to call it the sad circus look: so funny, you can't look away, so sad, you never forget it.

"Blow job lips."

Tina stops squeezing him and squints hard at the television.

"What? What did you say? I don't get it."

Billy turns away from her. He can feel the weight of the ashtray shift. His eyes are filling up. Marti. They were so close, closer than most brothers and sisters. After the sperm donator abandoned their mother, so did Marti (temporarily). She couldn't deal with all his crank calls and drive-bys, the control he continuously tried to exude, and the way their mother reacted to it. They would have been better off if he stayed away—their father, the sperm donator. When the bastard showed back up, struggling with sobriety, Marti, back for a spell herself, took their father in and let him dry out before returning home to his new family. Billy snorts.

"Oh, what is it now, Billy?" Tina's voice is mocking, turning a high pitch like a small animal trapped beneath a back porch. "Deanna? Is it Deanna again? I don't fucking believe this."

Of course, the old man started drinking again, dredging up musty pieces of a puzzle he and Marti long ago set aside. The gun was aimed at Billy mostly, but Marti jumped in front, took the verbal abuse, refused to believe the stuttering drunk. Billy saw him once at Marti's—wobbling in his work boots without laces, his stomach sloping toward the floor. Billy would like to see the old fuck get it up with nearly a whole fifth of Gentleman Jack swishing around his bloodstream. He is careful to make sure his face never resembles his father's slack, grizzled countenance.

Marti finally asked the sperm donator to leave, and after a dramatic farewell involving several broken lamps, the piece of shit stumbled out into the dark, and Marti, again, left straight behind him, just packed a few things and started the car, taking all the dark family secrets with her. Marti had saved Billy again.

"Fucking Deanna."

Tina leaps off the bed, and he can see her ass peeking out beneath the t-shirt. Most times, he would have been aroused and taken her right there. But most times (at least sober), he doesn't lie in bed in the early afternoon and cry for his sister. He knows he was never there for her the way she was for him. He can feel a dull thump growing from the back of his hands, through his arms, into his head. He thinks briefly of going into the motel bathroom and hanging himself from the shower rod, but he doesn't think it will hold. Maybe he could ask Tina to hold it up.

Billy opens his mouth to ask her and is surprised when a laugh heralds the arrival of new tears. His face feels hot and large. Was he really going to ask her? Tina is leaning her head against the window again. Billy moves as if to reach for her, sees her splayed chubby toes on the floor, and leans back against his pillows.

The letter is in a large manila envelope where he left it. It is 12:17 PM.

"Great. The Long Walk again. Jesus, Billy, what is wrong with you? Let it go." She spins from the window, and the stained curtains flap behind her like a cape. "What? You weren't going for the Long Walk again just now? What the fuck is wrong with you? No, what the Christ is wrong with me?" Tina marches to her overnight bag and rummages around.

Billy has seen this dance more than once. It only varies if there isn't a fresh pack. Then the Dance of the Angry Tina would commence and go a little something like this: Tina stomps off to the Stop and Go on the corner, the one made of mismatched cinder blocks covered in arcane drawings and burnt cigarette markings, stray cats slinking around the overflowing garbage bins, and upon her return, slams the door to get things rolling. The dance finale never varies, however, because Tina simply never goes away for good: she calms down, or not, and they have sex or argue or both until it is time to leave—Billy to return to his mother's basement and Tina to her apartment. Billy is sure her apartment must stink strongly of hair spray—he's never been there. Sometimes, if he doesn't wash his clothes before work, it is all he can smell in his cubicle: cat piss and hairspray. Billy absently sniffs the top of the blanket.

Tina finds a fresh pack of cigarettes, slightly squished down the middle, and holds them before her eyes triumphantly.

Thank God for small favors.

No cat piss at least.

"I don't want to hear about it, Billy. I've heard it a million times. Let it go." She climbs next to him, tries to reach between his legs again, but Billy twists, and she lunges for the ashtray before it can creep off the edge of the bed.

"Will you watch it, please?"

The letter is addressed to a woman, a Mrs. Somebody. It is still on the nightstand at 12:38 PM.

When Marti's apartment was broken into—when they were both living light years away from the moldy darkness of the family puzzle—Billy owned a little secondhand record shop in a low income part of town. Those were the good old days. Even their mother seemed to emerge from the torpor a damaged husband could drape over you. But the one who remained to carry on the family name—not doing too badly. The store was far from a success, but it was enough of one to make him feel like he was actually accomplishing something. Years in and out of college, trapped behind cubicles, nights spent staring at the space between a bottle of gin and a typewriter—over the instant he opened the doors every morning.

So Marti's place was robbed, and they took all her records but not the stereo for some reason—the old smudged black stereo the sperm donator had given them both many years ago. Billy didn't offer to replace her albums. He owned a goddamn record store in the city, and he did nothing. Marti came down and bought a few wholesale from him, just her favorites. She never called him on it. Marti moved back to Mondauk County after the store plummeted and finagled him a job at her new office.

"You know, Billy, if we could just get a place together. We could even get a little dog. No, a medium dog, like a retriever or something. We could do it, you know." She speaks between puffs of smoke. "With the money I make from the shop at night—and we're both due for a raise soon—we could be on very easy street. I can't keep living my life like this. I want a little kitchen and a medium dog."

The tears jump from Billy's to Tina's face, and he knows that she loves him in her own strange little way, in whatever way she is capable. She spent her life acting like the prettiest girl in town by being the easiest girl in town; he knows that much without her saying a word. She never mentions her father much either, but during a particularly rough night on a sea made strictly of ice picks (½ vodka, ½ sweetened iced tea, easy on the ice, stir once and chug), she spoke of his leaving when she was oh-so little. Her mother is a monster, fortressed behind an ever-present stain of an apron, her hair dyed the same color as Tina's, her every muscular twitch an anticipation of much prayed-for nuptials—for herself or Tina.

Billy reaches out to rub her hair, and it crunches in his hand.

"Marti lets you get away with all this shit." Her nose is running, smearing her lipstick.

True. Marti is tough and not very sentimental, but she indulges his sporadic crying jags.

Tina places her wet lips on his neck, and Billy can smell the stale smoke and the distinct smell of sex. What is he doing here? He doesn't love Tina—never will. It's just sex, someone to drink with, someone to fall asleep next to, someone to do all the filthy things he loves. But there is *always* a price to pay, Billy thinks, even between two consenting adults. It's wrong, and he knows it.

"We could get a dog, you know. It's in the stars, Billy. You can't mess with destiny." She speaks between sniffles; he can feel her snot running down his arm and his mind reaching for the envelope on the nightstand.

"It's like Marti doesn't know his family exists. How could she be this selfish? You have to be true." Billy's voice sounds strange in his mouth—thick.

He glances at the clock. The desk clerk told him the mail is picked up every day at two o'clock. Almost time to unveil the truth. Mail call for Room 14. Billy wonders if his uncle still owns the little handgun he once spied beneath the Christian pamphlets and Playboys in his nightstand. Billy wonders how it would feel in his mouth. He relaxes his head slowly until it hovers near Tina's shoulder.

"Bang. I'm dead," he whispers.

Tina smacks the top of his head and scrambles to escape his reach. The brown glass ashtray gives a little jump, and a few cigarette butts roll down the coverlet.

"Marti Marti Marti. Like she's so fucking smart. Let me go!" Tina lies still beneath the long reach of his arms. His face is now eye level with her bruise, feint brushes of days-old body wash reach his nose, and he realizes with a start he is becoming hard again.

"Funny, I thought I was dead."

"She's no saint, you know. Billy? Trust me, she's not. She just talks a good game."

True again: Marti is no saint. He never believed his little sister was, not even during the years when he routinely spit polished the pedestal he had erected in her honor. Their sibling friendship went through its moods like seasons, and even though currently a chill has settled between them, the tree itself never wore out. It has been that way since they were kids. Back when she was three and he was thirty, they used to say.

Growing up, as Billy became obsessed with all things musical, Marti became obsessed with love. She journeyed through her life and the lives of the men she consumed with a growing appetite for romance only found in old poetry, the more difficult the better. What she discovered, Billy thinks, is a shrinking aptitude for love. With time, Marti's romances grew increasingly complex and involved, as if like a junkie, the challenge bar needed to be set higher and higher each time, until the fall could possibly be fatal. During the affair, her suitor could do no wrong, and Marti would suffer no criticism. She believed every word they said.

Currently, Marti is sleeping with a significantly older married lawyer from the oh-so grand state of Alabama. Marti flies there to fuck him.

Billy presses his nose against Tina's bruise. If Tina is screwing someone else, he must have huge hands, Billy thinks. Tina doesn't require huge hands. For all her fleshiness and mouthiness and hair spray and Marlboro 100s, Tina requires small hands to massage her heart.

Outside the wind rattles against the window, and he can feel her stop struggling beneath him.

"There are other people involved, you know. The guy has kids. His wife—his wife has her own scent, her own way of laughing, a favorite position for sleeping. She's living and breathing, and just because the lawyer says it's dead, doesn't mean it's so."

He is talking against Tina's thigh and watching it vibrate as his volume increases.

"Remember when the German lady in accounting—remember when Marti found out she had been having an affair for twelve years. Marti thought it was romantic. Fucking pathetic if you ask me, to leave your wife and kids sleeping in Alabama while you bang some piece of ass barely out of college."

Tina's face is buried in her pillow. "Billy, let it lie. The queen will do whatever she wants to do, she'll have whoever she wants, and she doesn't care who's trampled in the process. When you're that pretty, it just comes easy, so she makes it harder."

"Tina, if you say another word about Marti, I will kill you in the bathtub." His words form bubbles over the bruise, and Billy imagines a little trapped tableau, like one of those Christmas shakers filled with snow, in it a lumberjack or the guy who installs the cable, pressing his large hands against Tina's legs as he takes her from behind against a nameless bar.

"…she just makes you feel stupid because you can't think—she's always talking. Marti hates my guts, but I keep her off your back."

He mumbles into the bruise: "…her turtle shell…."

And then Billy can't fight it anymore. The laughter peels back his lips and runs down Tina's leg. With her face buried in a pillow and his against her bruise, they sound like two suffocating Muppets arguing over the letter "C." Tina sits up, and Billy can see the smile, wide as a tunnel on her face. Tina doesn't know how to grin, and Billy laughs harder. Her eyes show concern and, yes, fear. Billy curls into a ball, his stomach seizing in cramps between gasping howls.

Tina pulls the coverlet back and climbs on top of him, hiking her t-shirt above her thighs. He pushes her off and pins her, trying to maneuver his underwear past his knees. Tina's breathing is clipped, little puffs of stale smoke. She bites his neck, and he screams out loud.

When he enters her, he thinks of his cousin: the down where her sideburns would have been if she were a boy, the way she always smelled like a sneeze—Elizabeth—supposedly staying only a few weeks with the family, when he and Marti were teenagers, until another relative relieved them of the load. He closes his eyes and thrusts harder. A sliver of light. Descending work boots. The tears. The fists. The lies. Marti hiding him behind a dumpster, the way Marti wouldn't look him in the eyes.

Tina is beating against his chest with her brightly colored nails, all sparkly red, curled into half fists. Billy opens his eyes. Did he fall asleep? Did he hurt her? His face is wet. He hopes it is sweat.

"Get. Off. Me." The tears are Tina's. "What the hell is wrong with you?"

He pulls the covers over his naked bottom half, underwear still down at his knees. He sniffs the backs of his hands to see if they smell like a sneeze.

"Deanna. Again. Christ. The fucking Long Walk? You think someone who reads books like you, a person who went to college like you would know better than to hang on to goddamn Deanna."

Billy reaches for her hand, his eyes crossing. That's what the basement in his parents' house had smelled like as a kid: a sneeze. Or was that only after Elizabeth took up temporary residency on the sofa bed down there, lounging about in a nightshirt? Was that part of the family puzzle? His heart feels like a broken record. And what the hell is Tina going on about? Why is she even here?

It is 12:52 PM.

"The Dark Lady?"

"I'm going for a shower. I can't put up with this anymore. Deanna doesn't want you. Deanna didn't know you existed until the party." Tina stands up and walks to her suitcase for a fresh Marlboro.

Tina is wrong, Billy thinks: the Dark Lady Deanna—a supervisor in another area of the same cubicle-infested hell ensnaring Tina, Marti, and himself—knew of Billy because of the fruit.

"Look at this ashtray. I promised my mom I would quit. Apparently, that's not the only thing," she says as she returns to the bed.

He brought Deanna a kiwi after he had noticed a fruit bowl in her cube. The Dark Lady accepted it with a loud "thank you" that somehow seemed like a whisper, before brushing past him and disappearing down a row of cubicles. Her after-smell was of warm spices, complimenting her naturally tan flesh and cropped dark hair. As she became one with the cubicles, Billy noticed the slight hunch of her shoulders the same way he made note of the muscles she used to force herself to smile. The next day he brought her two kiwis. He did this intermittently despite the complete absence of conversation. Billy was building a relationship.

When Billy finally found the voice to ask her for coffee and pie at a café featuring live music, her answer had been: "Not this time. I have a six year old."

Billy bought two tickets to a children's museum that night and left them on her desk the next morning, sitting between four apples, six bananas, and a kumquat. She never acknowledged the gift, but Billy was sure he was on the right path. A few days later, after dropping off a bag of plums, he told her: "It's okay, I was six once for a whole year." The Dark Lady, as she was known in interoffice mail between himself and Marti, stood up, arranged the new fruit to uncover her keyboard, and pushed past him to be swallowed by the cubicles again.

Marti warned him, told him to stay away. "She's been burnt, Billy." Pure propaganda, Billy thinks—he believes he is here to save Deanna, to waltz her into understanding the needs of her own heart. There is no doubt he is falling for the Dark Lady. How could Marti possibly understand? Marti never has to fight for anything in her life; men just make her acquaintance and then profess their love. Marti breathes it in and nourishes it until it no longer sustains her. What does Marti know about love?

Billy suspects Marti of subversion in the matter of the Dark Lady.

"The kids. Can you imagine the look on his children's faces when they find out? Marti's only two years older than his eldest. It's so selfish. This will affect everyone. Everyone. Doesn't she understand that? She's thinking like a guy, she's thinking with her—"

Tina punches the side of his head, and the ashtray finally fulfills its destiny and thuds to the floor. Patches of spotty red mask the dimples in Tina's cheeks.

"I'm leaving. I can't stand it anymore. You're obsessed with Deanna. And if I have to hear about fucking Marti…the two of you are both sick in the brain, you're both not right, you know that?"

Tina grabs the star charts in a bunch and shoves them into her bag. She seizes the clothes tossed about the room and smears a fresh line of red across her lips. Billy focuses all of his concentration on the letter. It is now 1:09 PM.

"I must be crazy in the head. You're a Scorpio for Christ's sake. You and Marti both. Find 'em, feel 'em, fuck 'em, and forget 'em." She heaves her bulging bag onto the chair and, after several attempts, finally manages to zipper it shut.

"Go ahead, tough guy, send the letter. Oh, you don't think I know what's in the letter? Yeah, the same way you think I don't know about the goddamn glass fruit you bought last week for Deanna. Are you a freak? Don't you know people laugh at you behind your back? Bad enough you wear a suit every day when everyone else is casual. No, you have to stalk a supervisor."

Billy stares at the letter, his mouth a small "O." Not for the first time, he wonders briefly if people could read his thoughts. How does she know about the little blown glass fruit?

"You'll ruin everyone's life. Who cares if he's a scumbag lawyer looking for a little tail? What's it to you? How does it affect your life? Go on, send the letter. Fuck with destiny. Mail'll be here soon."

Billy closes his mouth, and the scream echoes in his head. He shuts his eyes and curls into a little ball again, his hands clasped between his knees.

"They're going to fire you, you know. Karl told me. He wasn't supposed to, but I think he feels sorry for you because you're Marti's brother."

Billy forces the scream to stay inside his brain, but he can taste blood on his tongue.

Tina kneels by the side of the bed. "Billy, we gotta get outta here. C'mon, pack your things. Let's go, I don't know, let's go away. Let's just drive somewhere warm for a few days. The snow might keep the office closed for another day and if not, just call in your vacation days. Let's just go. You and me. No bars, no Marti, no office. You and me."

He squints between his lashes and can see her normally slack face tense and concerned. Little lines traverse her forehead, and Billy thinks he knows what she will look like when she is older. He opens his eyes all the way and releases his hands. Tina caresses them even though they are damp with sweat and swollen red.

"My bag..."

"It's right here. I'll pack it for you."

Using tissues, they clean up the cigarette butts and ashes. As they give a look around Room 14 and do a final check of their personal items, Billy thinks it wise to mention their current attire.

"We're not wearing any pants, Tina."

She drops the bag she is carrying and places her arms around his neck. He struggles briefly with the thought of strangling her but lets it go.

"Oh shit, I hope to God the Cuervo didn't break in my bag."

Tina rummages, then holds the bottle in the air.

"Unharmed."

"Shall we?"

It is 1:47 PM.

Tina pulls two shot glasses from deep within the pile in her bag, perches the letter addressed to Mrs. Somebody in some southern state or other on top. She kneels before the bag. Billy fishes the salt shaker from underneath the bed.

"The lemons are probably bad now."

"To us? Billy, to us?"

"To getting out of here." He grins and wonders if she sees the way his skin pulls over his skull like a Halloween mask.

"I'll drink to that!"

+

The sun has turned the sky pink, and the manila envelope is stained with interconnecting circles. They are sitting on the floor. It is 4:55 PM.

Tina paints her toenails a sparkly blue. Billy absently rubs between his legs.

"Do you remember when we met, Billy? The whole night was out of control. I thought you were going to kill me, remember? Outside in the car? The whole neighborhood must have heard us."

"You didn't think it was funny then."

"That was a good night. Never had sex like that. Leaves in my hair. My brains were all scrambled."

"*Take these evil lips and hold them fast...*"

"What's that?"

"Gene Pitney. Think the words are wrong though."

"No, don't know him."

Billy pours two more shots and drinks them both.

"They were playing that song at the office Christmas party. The Long Walk—right before it. The whole office was drunk, and they had that strange band. The singer had a handlebar mustache remember?—and a pompadour. Karl was trying to hit on Marti. Remember he was wearing the Santa hat?"

Tina stares at her feet, little lines moving in waves across her forehead. She begins to repaint her toes.

"Gene Pitney. Handlebar said it was ladies' choice, but I was too drunk to care. I couldn't watch Marti anymore. I couldn't drink anymore. And...there...she...was: Deanna. I walked right up to her. Remember? She wore that one piece black dress and a black choker: the Dark Lady."

Tina throws the polish against the television. It bounces and rolls under the bed.

"I asked her to dance. Just reached out my hand, bowed a little, and said, 'Will you dance with me?' Just like that. Everyone knew I was going to ask. You could tell because the whole place was quiet, and Handlebar was singing the right words, and the horn player was wailing. Asked her just like that. The whole Christmas party froze like in the movies, and I asked her, and my voice was cracking a little."

"No one stopped doing anything. I was there, remember?" She places her head between her knees, her eyes leaving her toes only to glance at the clock.

Billy ignores her. "Kept thinking how wonderful it would be. She smelled like spices. My hand just out there like that, everything still except my hand. I was shaking a little, see. And then...she...said... no. But she paused first, like she had to think about it. Her little clique wouldn't approve, she thought. I know it. She met my eyes. She said no. I wanted to say her name; I wanted to hear it in my mouth. I turned away and walked back through the crowd. Moses. That was me. They parted, and I started the Long Walk, everyone looking at me. I kept hearing her name over and over in my brain. Deanna Deanna Deanna. Everyone could hear it too. I could feel it in their eyes. But they didn't see the look, they didn't know what it meant, all that it held. Longest walk of my life."

Tina cries softly. There is enough in the bottle for two more shots. He offers the first to her.

"I know, Tina, I know. Sad, isn't it?"

Tina pours the drink down her throat and throws the shot glass at the television too, some rerun of a 70's show glaring pink from the screen. The glass shatters at the foot of the television, the bottom sitting proper, its one jagged piece a fang.

"I think we met a little before that, huh Tina? In the fall? At the little bar off Easton in Rhawnhurst—the Blue Comet—another office party? And here we are."

He crawls next to her, his drink in his hand. He is becoming aroused again.

"Guess I should let them know we're staying. They probably know. It's late. Is it still snowing?"

Tina looks at him. "Let's get lost here, okay? Let's just fuck and go to sleep."

Billy licks salt from the side of his hand. He remembers doing a tequila shot off Elizabeth's back once. Yeah, it was teenage lust—but it was pure. He should have slept with Elizabeth, he should have been her first, but in his family, Elizabeth was everyone's first. He wonders where she is. The night Elizabeth ran, after Marti hid him from their old man, Billy tried to cut his wrists but passed out. All he had wanted to do was be inside Elizabeth.

"The rest was just hell."

Billy finishes his tequila and climbs on top of Tina. He will take her on the floor, he thinks. He closes his eyes when he enters her, and for the first time, he thinks of nothing.

It is winter now; soon the spring and summer and, then again, the fall.

-end-

...no soul mates here...

"Is a dream a lie if it don't come true,
or is it something worse?"
Bruce Springsteen and the E Street Band, "The River"

Recommended Soundtrack:

"The River" by Bruce Springsteen and the E Street Band

"Hoochie Coochie Man" by Muddy Waters

"Suspicious Minds" by Elvis Presley

*H*e *would lie in bed and let the day cast over him like a shadow. She would be there midway between the tense struggle of a blanket of sleep and the drifting ice show of consciousness: mythical, a giant. His mind would remain in the dusty puddle between the two as well, lunging for the smell of her in bed, the thin line of hair leading down from her belly, the fold between her arm and side, the space where her thighs merged into the button of her tailbone cushion. It seemed to him a forever time; he was sure without her he would be beneath the air unable to even draw a breath. That was before. Now is a different time—and he wakes to her faint impression on the pillow next to his with a gasp.*

+

Shepherd reads the e-mail by accident. He slept late this morning, and the computer is on when he comes downstairs. Normally if Wiley leaves her e-mail open, he closes it and goes about his business. Today, he does the same. The final words of the exchange are before him a brief moment and then: gone. The screen stops flashing. The words in his mind do not: "...no...no soul mates here..."

Shepherd pauses on the way to the kitchen, listening for the padded paws of their dog. He wonders briefly if Wiley has taken the dog to the vet. "Duplicitous?" No answer. Maybe the dog escaped from the backyard when Shepherd crept down for a cigarette during the night. He had dreamt about the spinning wheel again and couldn't fall asleep until the sun opened the sky. No, the dog is Wiley's smoke detector; he would have heard if the dog were anywhere near him when he lit a cigarette. "Duplicitous?"

The dog appeared in their backyard two years ago, plump for a street mongrel, barking and running in circles. When Shepherd convinced himself to chase the animal out of the yard, the dog took flight the moment Shepherd's feet touched the grass. This became ritual for the next three days. On the third day, Shepherd opened the screen door and let it bang shut. The dog was gone instantly. It had been cold that autumn morning, and Shepherd went through the house top to bottom in an attempt to isolate the drafts. The doorknob to the basement was icy to the touch, and when Shepherd descended the stairs, bitter air bit into his skin. One of cellar storm doors was open, and two dog bowls were arranged on an old dishtowel. He returned to the first floor. Squatting on the kitchen tiles, Wiley was feeding the dog a banana. His wife looked up and smiled. Shepherd named him Duplicitous. The dog officially moved in that afternoon.

No dog, no wife, a good time for a cigarette, he thinks, but he smoked the last one during the night. He wants to write, to finish the short story that has been haunting him, nagging, for days—the one with the night-haired matron and her spinning wheel from his dream. The idea of turning on the monitor and seeing Wiley's exchange makes his hands shake, and he decides to masturbate instead. He climbs the stairs to their bedroom and removes the photographs from beneath his shaving kit. Shepherd locks the bathroom door. Maybe it was time for the dog's shots. "...no...no soul mates here..." Wiley glares at him from the top photograph, her forearm hiding her face, shielding everything but her eyes. The bar in the background is warm and inviting. He remembers singing Louis Armstrong to her while the piano player smoked imported cigarettes. Who is his wife's correspondent? Wiley spends hours in front of the computer screen, scanning photographs, designing logos, claiming to hate every second of her dalliance with e-commerce. Wouldn't Shepherd count as a soul mate? Where is the goddamn dog?

Shepherd finishes without realizing it and absently cleans himself. He thinks he hears barking in the distance, but the long whistle gives it away: it is the train. Shepherd walks down to the kitchen and fills a glass with ice. His zipper is undone. Sunlight bounces off the linoleum floor and reminds him of the last rays of a Sunday afternoon when he was a boy, the final glimpse of the sun before the darkness of another school week descended upon him. Shepherd zips his pants and goes to look for a cigarette.

+

Wiley is propped up by two pillows with her head buried in a collection of E. E. Cummings. She twists strands of her shoulder length auburn hair between long fingers, their nails chewed to the quick, wide eyes rapidly scanning the pages of the book. Shepherd is next to her, dressed in his pajamas, his slippers tucked under the bed. A draft plays with the curtains on either side.

"Where's the dog?"

"Hmmm?"

"The dog. Where's the dog?"

"Downstairs I think. The basement maybe."

He pretends to fall asleep, measuring the lengths of his breathing, stretching them until he feels he has achieved the desired result. Through lashed slits, he watches his wife's large brown eyes devour page after page of poetry. Her face registers nothing.

"Do you ever think of somebody else?"

Wiley, without looking up from her book: "Meaning?"

"Meaning are we happy? Are you happy?"

A page turns, and Wiley's shoulders give a slight quiver.

"I won't dignify that with an answer."

He stares at the top of her thighs, visible between her long t-shirt and the top of the blanket. Her thighs look warm. Shepherd shivers and pulls the sheet over his growing erection.

+

The witch is weaving again, her hair pulled tight like a raven's wing, exposing a jagged hairline. He can see her just out of the corner of his eye, the spinning wheel thundering between her legs. There is no other sound. In front of him, the room is empty. The space yawns beyond his sight line, and he wakes, shaking from the cold, the sheet and the blanket bundled up to his neck.

+

The first thing Wiley ever said to him was "shut up," and he was smitten from then forward. Benjamin caught sight of her initially: a collection of sharp determined lines in a Stetson hat and brown leather jacket, a knitted red scarf around her long neck, slouching toward the second-hand book shop in giant strides.

Benjamin was a large man with an even larger voice, raspy from too many cigarettes. Everything he said sounded like a shout.

"You're going to like this, Shep."

Her hair was choppy, her nose pointed, her whole face a cascading descension of angles. Her eyes were feral.

"Are you looking for anything in particular?"

She turned her eyes on him; he was trapped.

"Shut up."

Shepherd's mouth hung open. Benjamin stifled a laugh and went back to his newspaper.

"And close your mouth."

Shepherd did as he was told and leaned his back against a

bookcase, trying to catch Benjamin's attention.

Benjamin, opening his first sandwich of the day, his face close to the newsprint: "Don't look at me for help, Shep. You're on your own."

The woman paused in front of the poetry section and began running her fingers along the spines like she was playing a xylophone.

"We just got in an out of print copy of—"

"It's not for me. I hate poetry. It's a gift. I'll know it when I see it."

Benjamin, between bites: "Poetry is the language of love." Shepherd winced at his volume.

She snapped a hardbound collection into her palm.

"Price on the inside?"

"First page, upper right hand side."

Benjamin folded his newspaper and moved his considerable bulk away from the register. Shepherd squeezed behind the counter and fished out a bag.

"I don't need one, thanks."

"That'll be fourteen plus tax."

"What's your name?"

"Shepherd."

"Really?"

He handed her the change, careful to let his fingertips brush her hand. The woman pulled a colored pencil from her back pocket and bent over the open book, writing on the first blank page.

"I've changed my mind. No, keep the money. Credit for another time. My number's under the price."

Benjamin looked up from where he was pretending to inspect his lunch.

Wiley, like she was trying it out: "Shepherd."

He turned the book around and memorized the number just in case.

"You charge too much. Poetry's not worth the price."

"How do you know if you don't read it?"

"I know what I'm looking for."

"And that is?"

"I'm looking for words that burn."

Benjamin coughed into his sandwich.

"I'm a writer," Shepherd said.

"And I'm a Goliath."

Benjamin snorted back a mouthful of soda.

(Years later, Shepherd spent a week going through old books in the back room. He wanted to remember the name of the poet Wiley had rejected, but he could not.)

"What do you write?" she asked.

"Lies." Shepherd began to understand the game. Benjamin stopped chewing to better follow the exchange.

"Lies are better than the truth. Fiction is stronger than the truth. Fiction conquers," the woman said.

"What about writers who say they find the truth in fiction?"

Wiley tilted back her Stetson and smiled into Shepherd's eyes.

"Why—they're liars."

Much to Benjamin's chagrin, Shepherd hired her the following week. Wiley had been reluctantly finishing her graduate work in commercial design ("Too many Goliaths," she would say). And while she brought a fair amount of useful knowledge in regards to art books and nineteenth-century fiction, her frequent curtness and rapid-fire opinions alienated many a customer. Wiley began each sale by critiquing the purchases and wound up, more often than not, engaging the stunned buyer in a one-sided debate over the worthiness of the selection. Shepherd, doubled over with awkwardness (he could barely complete a sentence some days), couldn't bring himself to fire her, and despite Benjamin's animosity and insistent tirades, she never quit. When Shepherd finally asked her on a date some six months later, she answered yes before he finished the question. She quit the next day.

+

Wiley is up against two pillows; Shepherd undresses at the foot of the bed. A draft dances across the curtains like a wave unable to crash to shore. The point of Wiley's nose is pressed close to a worn paperback. Shepherd can make out Goethe on the spine.

"A little light reading?"

Wiley, without looking up: "I suppose."

Shepherd rubs his hands together. He spent a good portion of the evening hanging lost dog fliers on utility poles.

"Maybe somebody stole him. Why someone would want to steal somebody else's dog, I don't know. It's strange."

Wiley tosses the book on the floor and seizes his fingers in a bunch. She stares at his face and releases his hand.

Turning off the light and curling up, she says, "Happens to the best of us."

Shepherd hides beneath the bed coverings and presses his body against her back.

"We have a good marriage, don't we, Wiley?"

Wiley, without turning over: "Constant affirmation. Is this what you want?"

"Do you ever think of anyone else?"

"Do you?"

"No. I love you. I like the way things are; I like the way we are. I'm worried about Duplicitous though."

She curls her body tighter and says, "Then don't worry about things that don't need worrying about."

He moves away from her, and she adds, "I don't know what happened to the dog."

+

The threads of the spinning wheel start in color and turn black. Their ends flaying, they drift beyond his sight. He isn't floating, but he feels as if an invisible anchor he has known his entire life is now choked in rust and weathered from strain. The hellion is clad in night-sky from head to toe and never looks up from the wheel, never moves from the corner of his left eye. Faintly, a bass drum keeps an unvarying beat, and Shepherd hears a faceless laugh from his right, drifting up from where the floorboards should be. He thinks he can smell his father's cigarettes and the wine his mother always drank before she went to bed. More muffled voices and a final sharp laugh, and Shepherd can feel the weight of the space bearing down upon his bed, can sense the anchor giving way, can see the fine black strands trailing into nothing. The bass drum ceases, and the room rushes to meet him.

Shepherd's eyes open, and he can't breathe for all the air in his lungs.

+

"Love is an economy of motion," Wiley said. She took him to bed on their first date. He found her warm and hungry beneath her rough exterior. "Is this what you want?" she asked in clipped tones, puffs of words between labored breathing. Her nails played with the little hairs on the back of his neck. "Is this what you want?"

Benjamin stood for him at their wedding seven months after Wiley had quit the bookstore; his wife Lisa was the bridesmaid, their daughter Emily the flower girl. The hall was near empty. Wiley had invited no one. Shepherd had never met her friends; fact is, he didn't know if she had any. Once, after she'd moved in, an overseas letter arrived for Wiley. Inside was a photograph of a woman with very small hands wearing a knitted red scarf. An older man stood behind her, grasping her shoulders; they both wore silver wedding bands. "Angela," Wiley said to Shepherd—end of subject. A few years after their wedding, when the words had dried like curled missing-dog fliers, a second envelope was delivered via airmail. This time the picture was from a photo booth, and the man crowded next to the woman in the red scarf was decidedly younger and quite voracious, judging from the way his teeth appeared to have been sunk into her pale white neck. Her small hands were grasping his arm; she was still wearing a silver ring. Wiley read the words on the back and said, "She can look at herself in the mirror." Shepherd didn't ask any questions. Wiley never spoke of the woman or the note again.

In the bathroom before the ceremony, Benjamin drilled him: "Are you sure, Shep? You haven't been with many women. This is fast. This is really fast. Does she even like you?" He waved a flask in front of Shepherd's face.

Shepherd shrugged and passed his cigarette to Benjamin.

In Wiley, he found a similar sense of humor and a love for old jazz records. Wiley devoured every book Shepherd recommended; they would sit in corner bars, and Wiley would argue in angry tones over their interpretations and ramifications. While she rarely displayed any of the normal signs of affection in private, out on the town Wiley held his hand and whispered in his ear. If he was blue, Wiley would wait until he reached the zenith of his depression to touch the hairs on his neck and press his fingers into a bunch. "We'll get through it."

The only puzzle to Shepherd was that she would never say his name. She called him David.

+

spindrumspindrumlaugh(cigarette)spindrumspindrum(wine)spindrumspindrumlaugh
...and the apple is bitten bitten bitten into...
...and the apple is bitten bitten bitten in two...
spin DRUM spin DRUM spin DRUM
ceiling

+

Shepherd reads her e-mails while Wiley is at work. He pokes through her drawers and smells her dirty laundry, analyzes phone bills. He finds nothing more than business correspondence and an e-mail confirming the purchase of a Shakespeare bust that is more than likely a Christmas present. He makes a mental note to act surprised.

Throughout each day, the image of another man's penis inside his wife's mouth overtakes every thought and wavers just ahead of the next, twisting like a funhouse mirror.

The phone rings, and Benjamin booms through the wires.

"Still not sleeping?"

"No, the dream is awful. It's like being three again, and everything is bigger than you. The noises you remembered then: amplified tenfold."

A soft chuckle: "So, you're never going to close your eyes again?"

"No. I want to be alert. Short cat naps, that's it."

"Drink beers. Lots of them. I'm having one now, matter of fact."

"Do you ever have nightmares?"

"Me? No, Shep. I *am* a nightmare. By the time I'm done with the humping, I sleep like a kid."

"Poor Lisa."

"Hell, Shep. Woman snores like a son of a bitch. Gotta give her something to sleep on."

Shepherd reties the trash bag he's been pawing through and clears his throat.

"Ben E. Love, we've been friends forever, right?"

"As rain. Problem?"

"I think Wiley is falling in love with someone else."

"Jesus, Shep. Did she tell you this? Christ."

"No. I read something I shouldn't have. A letter. Part of a letter. An e-mail."

"What did it say? Did you confront her? Christ."

"It's not important. I asked her if she was happy. I can't tell her I read it."

Shepherd cradles the phone under his chin and opens the hall closet.

"We should talk. We should get together. Haven't seen you in a dog's age anyway. Why don't you meet me at the shop, and we'll go over to McCullough's for a few. I need some time away from the wife and kid anyway."

Shepherd stops going through Wiley's coat pockets.

"Shhh."

"What is it?"

Shepherd lets his ears take inventory of all the house sounds.

"Ghosts."

"Meet me tonight, okay?"

Nothing in the pockets but used tissues.

"Yeah. See you tonight. Bye."

Shepherd walks back to the kitchen with the phone. As Shepherd replaces the receiver, Benjamin says, "Hey, Shep. You find your dog yet?"

+

Benjamin started drinking during the day, as soon as they opened the shop in the morning. What began as a joke on slow days, a shot of liquor in the coffee, a ritual between two old friends, quickly became habit, and Shepherd saw his way out. Wiley was in advertising then, designing layouts for various magazines. Shepherd wanted to finish his novel, and Wiley told him the minute he stopped running, he would die; he took that as a positive. Shepherd sold his half of the shop to Benjamin, whose increased bulk rarely strayed from the stool behind the counter. The transition went smoothly, and Shepherd lent Benjamin a hand in finding a couple of part timers to stock the shelves and clean up after him.

The novel died a slow death, three chapters in a drawer, but his adeptness at the short form grew. Wiley never said a word about the book or the fact that he no longer earned a paycheck. The new stories were meaningless, silly romps, long on humor and innuendo but lacking the punch of what Shepherd considered serious fiction. Wiley read each of his short stories with a grim determination, and they would invariably have sex afterwards, wherever they were: kitchen floor, backyard, it didn't matter. Shepherd would undress as he finished the last page and frequently delivered the story with one sock on and his underwear around his ankles.

"Do you have to read it first?"

"Shut up."

"I'm dying here."

"You should write faster."

"You should read faster."

Soon the hours alone each day piled into each other, and Shepherd picked up smoking again, if only to have something to do between naps. However, when the short story well dried up, so did the sex. He tried to force them out, presenting Wiley with a page or two of lines, but he never had her on the basement steps again, and their nightly routine became just that: Wiley read a book, and Shepherd sneaked off to masturbate.

The morning after he first caught a glimpse of the gypsy woman laboring over the spinning wheel, he wrote about his father and the way his dad would never hug him, brushing his hairy knuckles over his son's forehead instead. Shepherd didn't show the story to Wiley. He didn't know why. Instead he left the pages sitting on the computer desk they shared. One morning, almost a week after its completion, he noticed the pages were out of order—he then began to write of the spinning wheel. The next day he discovered the words floating before he turned off the monitor: "…no…no soul mates here…"

+

Wiley is against a single pillow, the angles of her face tilting toward Rimbaud. The curtains stand stock-still. Shepherd drops to the floor and looks under the bed.

"Where's your other pillow."

Wiley's forehead creases, but her eyes remain on the book.

"I don't know."

Shepherd sits on the edge of the mattress to tie his shoes.

"What do you mean you don't know?"

Wiley glances at his face and says, "Maybe the dog has it."

"Funny. You're in bed early."

Wiley, annoyed: "I'm tired. Long day."

"I'm going to meet Benjamin."

"So you've said. You see I'm reading?"

Shepherd stands and stares at the curtains.

"I have to ask. I have to know, Wiley."

His wife slams the book shut and slowly raises her eyes to his, her fingers drumming an irritated tempo along the spine.

"Yes?"

"Did you give the dog to someone?"

"What the hell are you talking about?"

Shepherd runs his fingers along the edge of the curtains.

"Are you in love with someone else?"

"Jesus fucking Christ."

His fingers curl the bottom of the curtain, and he brushes it with the knuckles of his free hand.

"I found something, Wiley. Something I don't understand."

Wiley, jaw clenched, eyes unblinking: "Well, life's just full of mysteries, isn't it?"

Shepherd can feel his stomach rise to his throat, and he bunches the curtain into two red fists. The volume of his voice rattles the loose window.

"There's a reason why *sneak* rhymes with *weak*, Wiley."

Her face loosens, and he can see the Wiley in the photograph from the bar. She laughs and points at him.

"It's not funny."

Wiley, baring her teeth: "Well, it also rhymes with *meek*."

"What does that mean?"

Shepherd rips the curtain off the gold rings; he sees his face in the glass, his eyes rolling in their sockets.

"It means just that, David. What did you find? Confront me. Be strong for once. Fight for it."

His reflection wavers.

"Nothing, I found nothing."

"Oh, okay, so you come in here and accuse me? You tear down a curtain? Is this what you want? You want to hear that I met somebody on the Internet, someone I want to fuck? And that I'm sneaking around, sex-crazed, giving my dog away to some stranger? Is this what you want?"

The window swims in his eyes, and he steadies himself on the bedpost.

"I'm sorry. I just..."

He waits for Wiley's hand to crunch his fingers. Wiley opens her book.

"Go. Go meet your friend."

Shepherd leans over and stretches his fingers toward her hair.

"Just go."

"I'm sorry."

Shepherd touches his pockets to make sure he has cigarettes and leaves the room. Halfway down the stairs, Wiley's voice echoes from their bedroom.

"You will write again, you know."

+

He barely knows he is driving.

"All of this for nothing," he says aloud.

The bar is packed, but Benjamin finds a booth near the back door.

"No one sits here 'cause of the draft. Doesn't bother me. Two shots of Tullamore and a pitcher of beer. Shep?"

"Gin."

Benjamin, as the waitress walks away: "Did you see the ass on that? Christ."

"It's nothing, Ben. The whole thing is in my head. I haven't slept for four days, and maybe I'm not thinking straight."

"Come to papa," Benjamin says and finishes the shots before the waitress sets down Shepherd's drink. Benjamin turns the empty glasses over and snags the girl's apron strings as she walks away.

"Two more, hon, alright?"

The waitress pulls her apron back.

"And leave the empties. I like to count them."

The woman cocks an eyebrow toward Shepherd, and he shrugs in return.

In two hours time, eight empty shot glasses are arranged like a sun, and Benjamin's head wobbles when he speaks. Shepherd is working his way through his fifth gin and finishing his umpteenth cigarette.

"I made a fool of myself is what I did."

Benjamin raises his big hands in the air.

"A man has to take what's his sometimes, Shep. No shame in it."

"I tore a curtain. Just left it there. And she said the nicest thing when I left."

"We have urges, we have needs, we are easily led because of those needs. That's the burden of a man, Shep."

"Things have been distant, so maybe I can't be faulted for dreaming up stuff like this. If she won't read, then we won't do it on the floor, but I can't show her because—"

"Now I'm not saying Lisa doesn't have her moments of clarity, but she needs to understand that what a man needs, a man will go and find if it's not there in the marriage. This, Shep, this is an undeniable truth."

Benjamin punches the table, and the sun splinters into little disconnected satellites.

"She mocked me but I had it coming. The whole derisive laugh bit and yeah, she said, I'm doing some guy I met on the computer. I felt so small."

"Christ, I fucked things up. God's law? What do I know? Christ, society's law. I couldn't stop myself. I can't stop myself," Benjamin says.

Shepherd sips his drink then drops the glass on the table. An ice cube skids to the edge and glistens there.

"Wait. Wait. I never told her. I didn't even mention the computer. I never said a word about the goddamn computer. Oh, I'm going to throw up. She met someone on the computer. She fucking told me. Oh God. He's *writing* to her. She's *reading* his e-mails. Oh God. My wife is having sex with someone who seduced her with *e-mails*. Wiley is fucking somebody else's *words*."

Shepherd grips both of his own wrists, and his breath comes and goes in hiccups.

"And now, I don't know what. A hospital? Jail? How do you recover? How do you fix what you broke? A man's urges lead him, Shep. Christ."

Shepherd releases his wrists and watches Benjamin hide his face behind his hands.

"A hospital? Jail? For Wiley? What are you talking about?"

Benjamin uncovers his eyes and scrapes his palms down his stubble.

"Emily."

"Oh Jesus, what's wrong with Emily? Ben?"

"It was the night I checked in on her 'cause I thought she was sneaking on the phone, talking to the boys who always hang around now—like they can smell it. I told her: no phone after nine o'clock. If I told her once, I told her a thousand times. And she was sleeping, but the blankets, they were around her ankles, and I could see her thighs. Christ, they grow up fast. One minute they're little girls and the next, bang, they have their periods and all the rest of it. I couldn't sleep that night. You know how it is. Couldn't stop thinking of her thighs, creamy white, they were. Still had baby fat on 'em but shaped like a woman's. Goddamn it. Then she walks around in the morning in these one-piece nighties, and you can see her nipples, and you can't look away. I told her, I told her no one walks around this house naked. Told her to make sure she's dressed when she comes downstairs. And goddamn Lisa. Yeah, I like to go to a bar after I close shop, what's it to her, you know? I come home, and she's sleeping, and a man has urges, Shep. Christ, you know. What am I telling you? You know. So I start checking on Emily every night when I come home, pretending like I'm tucking her in. She even says, 'I'm too old to be tucked in,' but I know she likes it, the attention from her old man. And one night she can't sleep, some bad dream or other, and I'm just in from the bar, and goddamn Lisa is asleep and snoring. Christ, that woman can snore. So I tell her, I tell Emily that her mother used to rub my back when I couldn't sleep, and I say maybe if I give her a massage, she'll fall asleep. And she goddamn turns on her stomach just like that. Her nightie's all bunched up, and I can see her bottom peeking out of the little white underwear. So I tell her to take the nightie off so I can rub her back, make it easier, you know. And she does it, *just like that*. And I rub her. I rub her entire body, and she was shaking, but I tell her it's okay, hey, you know, it's just me, and we have to be quiet so your mother doesn't wake up. Lisa's snoring to beat the band but still: a man has to be careful. And now I go in every night. I tuck my daughter in every single goddamn fucking night."

Benjamin exhales and shakes a few drops from a shot glass into his mouth. The sliver of ice slips off the table. Shepherd feels the room spin and uses the table to leverage himself to his feet.

"Benjamin. Benjamin, she's twelve. She's twelve."

"Don't I know it."

Shepherd stumbles out the back door, and the cold air makes his head snap back. A train whistle sounds just beneath the cry of the wind, its wheels thundering on the tracks like a bass drum. His car seems to be very far away, and when he opens the door, he vomits on the dashboard.

+

Wiley is stretched out across the entire bed, and Shepherd undresses in the hallway so he doesn't wake her. His fingers smell like gin. The last curtain billows without rest. Wiley is asleep on top of the covers. Somewhere outside a dog barks then whines and stops. Shepherd climbs into bed and buries his nose in his wife's hair and tries to let the perfume of her shampoo erase the smell of the bar.

-end-

Stories of Abuse

She Said

"Jesus died for somebody's sins but not mine."
The Patti Smith Group, "Gloria/In Excelsis Deo"

Recommended Soundtrack:

"Gloria/In Excelsis Deo" by the Patti Smith Group

"Pennyroyal Tea" {live unplugged version} by Nirvana

"The Slim" by Sugar

yesterday, I found something dead; what can I tell you?
      I want you to understand; well, how old am I? what?
nineteen? and, oh, I have four scars, descending: numbers
      two and three are kind of special, but, well, is it art?
it happens every year and they fall: the leaves, I mean;
      well, I try and catch one just to see if it screams, like
a snowflake dissolving on a pink tongue; my daddy denied
      himself this pleasure and maybe *that* explains everything.

yesterday, I touched something dead by the wishing well;
      what can I tell you? I had a lover once who chased the sun,
but he fell too; and, oh, I once kept a thirsty rabbit in
      a dusty cage when I was four, and my daddy hid the remains;
I cried and he came (and another leaf found its way) and I
      was touched but I could not feel (and, no, I'll never tell).

yesterday, I smelled something dead by the wishing well,
      under the hanging tree; well, what can I tell you? I *need* you
to understand; I never saw the ocean, but once in the rain
      I looked for him, running, and I scratched myself a barren
ditch to catch *all those leaves*; then, you know what I did?
      I crawled on all fours sniffing for him behind the place where
he made me quiet, and I heard another limb sing his weight.

yesterday, did I tell you? I felt something dead beneath
      the pile on the lawn, and I ran under the hanging tree to catch
a leaf, but each one creates a tiny pulsing blur, a river ripe
      and red and barren (did I mention it was my birthday?), and
every time I open my mouth, I masturbate my mind; well, what
      can I tell you, love? I always hated October.

yesterday, I kissed something deep and dark and dead and dry
    under the pile, and you didn't seem to mind; well, what can
      I tell you, Daddy? the trees are shaking and the well is
empty, calling you to echo your own needs; and we look
      toward the earth and fall and dig, endlessly.

Bailey's Story

"I gather speed from you fucking with me."
Pearl Jam, "Rearview Mirror"

Recommended Soundtrack:

"Rearview Mirror" by Pearl Jam

"Everybody Knows" by Leonard Cohen

"Babe I'm Gonna Leave You" by Led Zeppelin

Neve will never believe this.

"In a circle. Everyone. Okay? Trina, light the candles. In a circle. Everyone? Okay?"

That's Mrs. Anastasio.

They are already in circles, spiraling around the low coffee table, too many to fit. Circles break upon each other and merge; others are satellites around the larger configuration. Bailey thinks it is hard to see the center, but the center, of course, is Trina: on the floor, back to the sofa, legs under the coffee table.

Neve will never believe this: they are in loose circles, and no one makes fun of Bailey. No one tries to trip her or make her sit in anything wet and squishy or giggles behind a hand. Even when she finds herself spacing out on the circles of which she is finally a part, not a single kid calls out, "dumb bunny" or "hey, Bailey, let us know when the shuttle lands!" like they do in algebra and chemistry and world religions. Even Mattie Mishkin and her self-proclaimed Bod Squad keep their disdain minimized to a few dirty looks launched from a distance within the inner circle. And to top it off, Mrs. Anastasio promised to read their palms before the night is over.

Led Zeppelin is trying like hell to quit somebody baby, and Bailey closes her eyes. *This is what different feels like. This is what different feels like. This is what different feels like.*

+

"Nikki loved this shit," says someone Bailey doesn't know.

"Uh-huh."

"She thought Trina's parties were the best."

"Uh-huh."

The girl Bailey doesn't know coughs and looks around the circle.

"Well, congratulations, Bailey. You made it to the big league."

"Okay."

It is Trina's birthday, and since it falls close to Halloween, Mrs. Anastasio can be counted on to throw a costume party. Bailey was never invited to one of Trina's birthday bashes before; fact is, she never hung out with any of the kids from school with the exception of Nikki, and Nikki moved away more than a year ago. Nikki had never missed a party and had never failed to fill Bailey in on all the details, her whispers carrying the sharp edge of Marlboros smoked an hour before school.

Trina is no longer in the center, and Bailey spaces out again. If she concentrates, she can zoom in on a conversation much the way she does while lying in bed listening to the monologues her father watches on the black and white that wobbles on a rusty dinner tray.

The boys, she listens to the boys:

"Who is she?"

"I don't know. Someone Trina knows, I guess."

"She's in history with us, right?"

"Is she the one who kissed…?"

"Who is she?"

Bailey opens her eyes.

She didn't count on the boys. Her experience with them resembled watching a wild life documentary on television; fascinating and untamed, the boys wandered the halls of school, pushing one another, making dirty jokes, forcing out belly laughs in what Bailey imagined were attempts to sound like their fathers. The boys ignored Bailey, thin and pale, short hair she cut herself, glasses perpetually sliding down her nose whenever she would sweat.

Bailey can't take her eyes off the boys.

"After Mom goes to bed, we're going to play spin the bottle."

Trina is whispering in her ear between nacho crunches; Bailey can smell beer behind the ranch dip.

"I was just looking at their costumes."

Trina brings her lips to Bailey's ear. Barbara Lochetta stares, chomps loudly on a potato chip, and leaves the room.

"Never kissed a boy before, huh? Well, it's okay. We'll talk later. It's easy."

Bailey's face burns, and she thinks of Jerry Lonergan from math class. Jerry is a year ahead of her, but he is behind in math. She hoped he would be at Trina's but if he is, he's hidden behind a mask.

"Hey, move closer Bailey. We're gonna Ouija."

+

Dear Bailey,

It is hard for me to write this, but I thought it would be easier than talking on the phone. I know we haven't been what you would call close during the past five years. Still studying art therapy? I wasn't even sure where you

lived until I asked Aunt Beady, and even she had to do
some detective work. I guess some things haven't changed.
You're still in hiding and this is what disturbs me. It's time
for the truth to come out, big sister. It's time for the games
to stop.

+

"That supposed to be some kind of yarmulke, Bailey?"
Mattie Mishkin.

The kids are all in costumes. Trina is a cheerleader for what one
girl says with a practiced sigh is a record fifth year. Trina's best friend,
Barbara Lochetta, is Fay Wray from the King Kong movie. You can
see her boobs jiggling beneath her toga; all the boys are saying so.
Bailey doesn't want to look just in case. Bailey sewed her witch's cape
from scraps she found at her aunt's house after the invitation arrived.
Her hat is more slanted than pointed, more Italian gondola driver
than sinister witch, but she ran out of material; so excited at being
invited, she used almost every inch of the black cloth for her cape.
Neve warned her that it was a trick, the invitation, and Bailey would
find herself at the butt end of some serious shit, but Bailey ignored
her. She had no idea why she'd been asked to come to the party, and
at that moment, she didn't care.

Trina hands her glass to a boy dressed as an ape and snatches
Bailey's witch hat. Led Zeppelin is breaking hearts and saying it is
time to go.

"The color this fall is black, and all hats will resemble the leaning
tower of pizza."

Trina approximates a runway walk and tosses the hat back to
Bailey.

"Make it yourself? I think you did a great job, Bailey."

Bailey stares at her worn sneakers, and Mrs. Anastasio lights the
remaining candles. Barbara Lochetta and Mattie Mishkin catch each
other's eyes, and Bailey suddenly is sure the boy in the ape costume is
Jerry Lonergan.

+

You have to understand this: you understand nothing.
You cannot blame Daddy for your lack of popularity in
high school, the fact that you never had any boyfriends, or

whatever dead end job you currently have. This is
something all the judges and cops in the world seemed to
grasp, but you could not. Maybe you expected too much.
There aren't many heroes left in the world, Bailey, as I'm
sure you understand now. You may have thought you were
being brave, you may have believed you were doing the
right thing, but no one becomes a hero because they want
the job; it is thrust upon the person, and they have to make
of it what they can.

+

"You have to move so we can clear off the table."
Barbara Lochetta.

Trina and Barbara aren't like the others; they never make sport
with Bailey or hide her glasses when she falls asleep in English. Trina
and Barbara went to grade school with Bailey and Nikki, as did many
of the kids at Trina's party. In seventh grade, after Mattie Mishkin
and the nascent Bod Squad found Bailey sleeping in a corner by the
convent during recess and proceeded to cover her uniform with
phlegm, Trina walked between them, yanked Bailey's hand, and
pulled her free. Bailey tried to thank her, but Trina was already on the
move, a look of disgust on her face. Bailey wasn't completely sure
that it wasn't directed at her.

"Huh? Oh, okay."

The baskets of chips and pretzels disappear, and Bailey backs
herself against the fake fireplace. Mattie Mishkin whispers to a girl
dressed as a safari hunter, and they both giggle in Bailey's direction.

Jerry Lonergan.

Tutoring is Bailey's only extra-curricular activity. She tried out for
track, but after Mattie Mishkin hung Bailey's tattered underwear (the
pair with the large hole on the left side) in the boys' locker room
before the end of the first practice, Bailey quit. Mrs. Weller offered
Bailey a position as a tutor. The teacher pulled her aside after math
class and told her she knew what Bailey was going through and
sometimes all it took to break in was to grab the bull by the horns.
Mrs. Weller always looked at Bailey with puppy dog eyes, and once,
Bailey was sure they were filled with water.

The boy in the ape mask is now on the sofa.

Jerry Lonergan was her first tutoring student. Gone was the boy
with the strutting walk and the eyes that looked over your head when

you spoke to him in the hallways or the parking lot, as if a more interesting engagement was pressing upon him—replaced by a boy whose straight brown hair fell in his eyes when he concentrated, a boy who did not know when to stop staring and who stuttered a little when they weren't discussing homework. Neve told her to forget about Jerry Lonergan, but Bailey could do nothing but the opposite. Another Nikki, Neve said.

The boy in the ape mask is now leaning against the wall next to the fake fireplace. Bailey feels her pulse jump, and she reaches for the headband in her pocket.

+

"Ouija time. Come on. All of you. Trina, a veggie cocktail, will you?"

Mrs. Anastasio.

Trina's mom is wearing a long blue robe and large colored jewels on her fingers. Bailey doesn't know if this is a costume or if Trina's mom dresses like this every day. She thinks she can smell beer on Mrs. Anastasio's breath too. Trina smokes with her mom; maybe she drinks beer with her as well.

"Everybody has a turn. Gather round. Barbara, the lights already."

The room goes dark except for the candles. Bailey makes sure she can see Mattie Mishkin across the room. The boy in the ape mask is gone.

"You know how this works. You two. Barbara and you. Put your fingertips on the pointer. Real light. Good. Now we're gonna ask it some questions, and the Ouija will answer. Close your eyes, Barbara. The only question you don't ask is when you're going to die, okay? That's not a good question to ask."

"How about when we're going to get laid?"

"Tommy, with those braces, I don't think the Ouija's gonna be able to help you much."

The kids laugh and so does Tommy. Bailey allows herself a smile. Neve was wrong; this is fun. All her life, Neve told her they were different—bad different. Bailey always thought it was because they didn't have a nice car like the Lochettas or go to Florida every summer like the Anastasios. But Neve was wrong. This is different and different is good.

"Afterwards, I'm going to read your palms. So Tommy, make sure you don't do nothing with yours while we Ouija, okay?"

Bailey shuts her eyes.

+

When Mom left, the whole tone of the house changed. Daddy tried, but he drank too much. He worked too hard to give us a decent house, and he drank too much. Hopefully you see now what you did not see then. But yours were not the happiest high school years ever known, were they? You locked yourself in your room with that headband and let the house go to pot around you. I know it was a lot to take on, but we did okay for a few years, remember? Then Nikki left, and you closed your bedroom door for good. End of story. Well, you may think you opened the door for all to see, but it's time for the whole truth, Bailey. It's time for two sisters to square with the past. It's only fair and it's not easy.

+

"What's your story, Bailey?"

Barbara Lochetta in school the day before yesterday.

Barbara was walking the hall toward Biology Lab, and Bailey was standing in the doorway of study hall fingering Jerry Lonergan's scarf. Jerry had left it after their last tutoring session the day before, and Bailey was going to return it to him if only because Neve caught her with it and told her one talisman in the house was enough. Bailey thought Barbara's tone rather ominous. She dropped the scarf and walked to the lab, her eyes on her scuffed black and white saddle shoes.

"You have to ask your question out loud."

Mrs. Anastasio in her living room right now.

"What's it going to be, Bailey?"

"Will Jerry Lonergan take me to the prom?"

Someone imitating Bailey's soft sing-song voice.

All the hairs on Bailey's neck jump, and Barbara Lochetta stiffens.

+

I can't live with the lies, Bailey. I want a face to face if you can stand it. I want us to look each other in the eye and talk about what happened. The damage has been done, and it is time to piece our family back together. I know I haven't been exactly the most understanding person, but considering the trial and everything that went with it, I believe my initial reactions were based more on shock than anything else. I have accepted the truth, as hard as it was to swallow, and I want you to do the same.

+

"Nothing's happening."

Trina.

"Maybe we should just move on to the palm reading. You, let me see your hands."

Mrs. Anastasio's hand is soft; it feels like silk. Bailey tries not to think about everyone's eyes looking in her direction or the rude noises rising from the Bod Squad.

"Your hand is so rough. Do you like to work in the backyard, Bailey? Now, palmistry is an art. I can tell a lot about your character, your future, your love life from studying the lines and swirls in your palm."

Mattie Mishkin snorts, and someone tells her to be quiet. Bailey stares at her palm. Mrs. Anastasio's breath is acrid, and Bailey wonders if she could become drunk just by breathing it in.

"Are these possible futures?" she asks Trina's mom. "Or are these things that are really going to happen?"

"My dear, every future is possible. A good palm reading shows you how to understand your choices before you make them. The decisions are yours to make. The truth is all that matters. Now this line, this is your love line. This line is strong until here—see where it breaks off. Heartbreak. Do you have a boyfriend, hon?"

More snickers from the Bod Squad. Bailey pulls her hand away. Mrs. Anastasio sways a little and leans back on the couch.

"Mom, let's get back to the Ouija, okay?"

Trina's face flashes angry in the candlelight.

Bailey and Barbara Lochetta place their fingers on the pointer. Mattie Mishkin is looking over Bailey's shoulder; Mattie's body shakes, and she covers her mouth with her hand.

"Trina, be a dear and make Mommy a veggie cocktail."

"In a second. Okay, think of your question and concentrate. Just let your fingers barely touch the surface of the pointer, Yeah, like that."

A window shakes in the dining room, and Bailey wonders what Nikki asked the Ouija.

+

"No, it's fun. It doesn't mean anything. Here, chew some gum."

Nikki a long time ago.

"You have to learn sometime."

Nikki's tongue slid into Bailey's mouth, played along the molars, her arms around Bailey's neck. Bailey could taste cigarettes; she counted Nikki's heartbeats.

"See, no big deal. This is what we do when we have a party. You pick one boy, and you kiss all night."

Bailey pulled Nikki closer, and Nikki pulled away.

"You'll be a pro in no time."

Nikki went home, and Bailey laid in bed, forcing herself awake as she did every night, just in case. Her body tingled when she thought of the kiss. She planned to ask Nikki to show her more the next day.

When she arrived at Nikki's after school, Nikki kept talking and showing Bailey photographs of all the boys she kissed at parties. Bailey tried to hold her hand, but Nikki swung underneath her arm and went to the bathroom.

"You have to be quick," she said on her way out.

Before Nikki returned, Bailey stole her sweater and wore it every day for a week. Nikki stopped eating lunch with her and pretended she wasn't home when Bailey knocked. Nikki's mom had to call Bailey's house to ask her father for the sweater back. Neve said it was an embarrassment to the entire family. Neve said Mom would have had a bird.

Nikki moved away at the end of the school year and never answered the letters Bailey mailed to the old address, one a day, hoping they would be forwarded. Nikki's dad got a new job in Florida. Neve told her Nikki moved to escape Bailey's clutches. Bailey believed her.

+

My clearest memory of you is when we were little and Mom took us to the see the circus, and she bought us both stuffed monkeys. You had your nose pressed against the glass of the monkey cage, and you kept lifting your stuffed animal high into the air so everyone could see you had a monkey right there. I remember yelling at you and trying to throw away your stuffed animal. I remember not wanting to stand out. When I think about that day at the circus, I realize it was the first time I felt the gulf between us. I wanted everything to be normal, just like everyone else's family. You wanted to be different. You always wanted things to be different, Bailey, and now they are.

+

"Is it yes?"

Led Zeppelin has stopped singing, and Bailey can hear everyone breathing, can feel the crowd around her like a giant beast, exhaling and inhaling. Someone is sitting very close to her back, rasping through a Halloween mask. Bailey feels her question rattle through her brain:

Could everything be different? Could everything be different? Could everything be different?

The pointer inches with a squeak.

"Is it yes?"

"Shhh."

The pointer lurches toward the affirmative, and the room gasps. Mattie leans forward, and the candles go out.

The monologue is over. A beer tab snaps.

-I should just stay here this time.

She smells her mother's headband. The scent is gone. It is just a headband.

-I can't do it again, Mom. I can't. I'm sorry. Let Neve do it.

The steps creak, three and five, like they always do when he tries to be quiet.

-Please please please. Dear God, please let it happen to Neve tonight. I'm so tired. I'll do anything. Please.

A grunt at the top of the steps, and the bathroom door being opened, and the sound of someone pissing. Not someone. He never flushes.

-Hail Mary, full of grace, the Lord is with Thee, blessed art Thou among women and—

A doorknob turns. Neve's.

She pulls the headband under her nose, and her mother is there: the lilac scent of the perfume she and Neve bought for her at the Five and Dime—the somehow welcoming smell of her mother's sweat when she came in from pulling weeds—and underlying it all: a familiar fragrance of fear.

She pulls back the covers and steps into the hallway. His back is to her. Neve's door is open.

-In here, Daddy.

He turns to her, and she can't make out his face.

"Jesus Christ!"

Barbara Lochetta and someone else screaming behind her.

The lights are back on and still someone screams.

"Trina, get a washcloth. Get the hell away from my curtains. That's not funny. You could have hurt yourself climbing through the window. Trina, get some ice in a washcloth."

It happens very fast: Jerry Lonergan's lips are inches away from Bailey's face. Two boys climb into the house and close the dining room window behind them, exchanging guilty looks with Mattie Mishkin. All the masks are off; everyone's eyes are wide. The screaming continues. Barbara Lochetta runs up the stairs and a door slams. Jerry Lonergan puts the ape mask back on and then takes it off. Trina whispers something, and the two boys follow her into the kitchen.

"That was fucking great! That was scary!"

Mattie Mishkin between gales of laughter, holding on to someone dressed as an altar boy.

"Couldn't they just hide in a closet? I mean, a window—my God, Trina. Where's my cocktail, hon?"

Bailey closes her mouth, and the screaming stops. Trina is washing Bailey's hands. There is blood on the washcloth.

"Just a prank, Bailey. I'm sorry. We didn't mean to upset you. We do something like this every year. Someone jumps out and puts a fright into the gang."

Bailey looks down and her palms stare back, half-moon slices winking at her from where her nails tore into her love line. Everything *is* different. She knows what she has to do.

+

Please write back. It's the end of the lies. You have put Daddy and the rest of the family through enough trouble. It's time to open our hearts and let Jesus do the rest. Ours was not the happiest childhood, but Daddy did his best, more than most would do. Your anger turned to lies and your lies to hate. And no one believed you. They saw the truth, Bailey: a good man who drank too much but who wouldn't touch a hair on his children's bodies. He still loves you.

It took me a long time to realize this, but I still love you too.

You can't change the past, but you can alter your future. I pray for you every night, Bailey.

Love, your sister,
Neve

-end-

When Aunt Mel Died

"You don't make up for your sins in a church.
You do it on the streets. You do it at home.
The rest is bullshit and you know it."
Charlie in *Mean Streets*

Recommended Soundtrack:

"America" by Simon and Garfunkel

"Maybe I'm Amazed" {live version}
by Paul McCartney and Wings

"Break On Through (To The Other Side)" by the Doors

" Aunt Mel died." My mother says this as she leans over me and kisses my cheek. It is an early autumn morning, and my head throbs the drum beat of another wrestle with a bottle, maybe several bottles. I am lying in the guest bed in my parents' house. "You can stay here if you want. I'm going to the hospital," my mother says. The guest bedroom is an immaculate collection of modern furniture set amid soft yellow that hurts my eyes. I arrived last night to visit, or so I said. I was out of booze, and the stores were all closed. I wound my way through my parents' meager liquor cabinet while watching an old Ingrid Bergman film on their basement television, sneaking outside for quick drags on a few stale cigarettes I had found in my leather jacket the day before. I managed to stay away from their bathtub, although I have a faint memory of peeing in it before collapsing on the guest bed.

Aunt Mel was called Mel because that's what my late uncle called her. No one remembers why. She was a strong, healthy woman, a maternity nurse who would routinely carry two babies over each shoulder to walk off their night cries. A popular story in my family goes like this: one shift found Aunt Mel in the care of a very small baby with a curious yellow complexion. All evening my aunt walked the baby back and forth across the maternity ward. She was aghast the previous shift had not made notation of the child's illness. Undaunted by reprimand (Aunt Mel considered doctors a notch above lawyers when it came to common sense, the only true currency of her generation), she began to administer oxygen to the little jaundiced baby. The baby remained yellow. At dawn, Aunt Mel marched to the head nurse, barely allowing the poor woman to remove the scarf from her hair. After much agitation (mostly on Aunt Mel's part), it was revealed the baby was black; his parents were African-Americans of light complexion. Aunt Mel told the story in tight, clipped tones, her thin lips never cracking as much as a grin until the punch line. "Somewhere, there's a little boy with so much oxygen in him, he floats," she would say as a finale, and a riotous boom of a laugh would commence and not cease until her entire audience was doubled over.

I go to the bathroom, thinking of Aunt Mel, trying not to think of Casey. I can hear my mother downstairs on the phone. "...no, what with...I don't think he should go either...I told him he can stay here...he's asleep...no, I have to leave...okay, bye." I wait to flush the toilet until I hear her car pull out of the driveway, agonizing through the minutes by listing every Beatles song from every Beatles album (in order) just so I don't look at the tub.

+

Casey wasn't born wrong, she was made, or so the popular school of thought went. She spent much of her young adult life in and out of mental hospitals; she was a cutter, among other things. Casey would carve her arms and her stomach with intricate circles and slashes. A lifetime of abuse and neglect left her with a running commentary of voices in her head, or so she described. A childhood of mysterious, unexplained absences from school left her without any real friends. She floated from crowd to crowd in her early twenties, partially so her trips to the hospital would not be noticed, but mostly because she didn't belong anywhere in particular. Casey's parents (divorced and both remarried) kept their distance but continued to carry her on their insurance as long as they could. Bystanders in her abuse, they wore the forced smiles of the overly guilty. Casey would say she was born of the moon only by happenstance; the sun was her true parent, and she waged a long war to reach home again. "I am of the sun," she would say to me with a wink, "and I burn so bright."

We met at a party I didn't want to attend, some college thing at somebody else's college. It was early October. My friends coerced me during one of my frequent sabbaticals from school, when I would wander from job to job, obsession to obsession, trying to find my way. My friends' hypothesis was this: if I became social in their college crowds, I would resume my studies. The idea of an English degree hanging on a wall while beneath it I scribbled story after terrible story on yellow legal pads held no interest for me. I was without a path.

Casey was seated at the far end of a long kitchen table nursing a salty dog. Revelers would wander in and spare a few words in her direction. When they left, which was soon (Casey was not one for social mixing), she would shove a cheese cracker into her mouth and cover her face with a hand while she finished. I first noticed her scars during this bizarre ritual—I couldn't help but see them despite a long sleeved shirt and many dangling bracelets. The scar tissue appeared red and throbbing and just the starting point. She was the prettiest girl I had ever seen.

I watched her all night. When my friends' liquor-fueled activities signaled a quick escape was in order (one was ensconced in a bedroom with the acne scarred, frizzy-haired host, the rest attempting a rescue), I entered the kitchen, cool as a cucumber, moved the basket of cheese crackers to the other end of the table, and then exited. A few minutes later, leather jacket on, gripping house keys in my pocket, I leaned in the archway of the long kitchen. The basket of cheese crackers was again beside its secret admirer. I smiled. "Your move, Ace," she said, and I left the party, reluctantly now, with her phone number and a kiss tasting of cheddar cheese. We went to the movies the next evening and talked and smoked our way through it. I slept with her the night after on my brother's bed. (I was staying with him, unable to afford a place of my own.) Two months later Casey and I rented an efficiency apartment behind a steak sandwich shop. While Casey attended college, I worked a streak of odd jobs to pay the rent and pretended to write. I was never happier in my whole life.

+

"Good to see you," says a second cousin, the one with a beard whose name I can never remember. I tried to enter the church quietly through a side door; I didn't want to sit with my parents and brother. The cousin with a beard catches me and shakes my hand until I think it will break. He wears the funeral smile, the one with the upraised eyebrows and tilted shoulder. I escape his grip and find a pew near the back.

The casket is rolling up now, castors squeaking like tiny field mice trapped beneath a porch. I don't want to hear anything; I try to block out the mice propping up Aunt Mel by replaying an unwritten short story. But I know I won't write tonight or the night after or even the one after that.

My cousins are all of a healthy build, square jaws, tight lips, steady unwavering eyes. They have good careers and are all engaged to extremely bright and pretty blondes with quick wits. I am from a somewhat lesser stock. My skin sags on my face as if it doesn't like the fit, and I tend to sweat my way through shirts ten minutes after getting dressed. Like my cousins, I am relatively thin, but their muscles contrast sharply with my flabby stomach and shapeless arms. I have their green eyes, that is all. Even my brother, enjoying the swinging lifestyle of the recently divorced, towers over me in career achievement as well as physical stature. My mother's first husband, my biological father, was a slovenly man with no taste for anything that didn't arrive in a can. I am sure I look just like him.

The funeral follows the paths of other funerals, and the readings by my cousins are both heart wrenching and ragged. There is a bagpipe player standing near the rear of the church, waiting for his cue to begin the exit procession. I can see the backs of my parents' heads as they nod in all the right places. From the left side of the church, a little girl with a head of golden curls, daughter of one of my cousins no doubt, races up the aisle toward the vestibule. The congregation hears the heavy doors creak open slowly and slam shut, and I am back at Casey's funeral. I focus on a candle until the moment passes, but I know it never will. Casey's funeral is not a rerun, not an old movie you view with distance and foreknowledge. It is happening now. It is the present, and it will never cease being new.

+

As much as our daytime lives differed, we became one every night. Sitting together at an old wooden table, leaves down, the Doors erupting from the stereo, we swallowed shots together ("ashes to ashes, funk to funky," our battle cry), and Casey spun the twisted yarn of her life into something resembling a linear progression. Born poor, her parents were barely functioning alcoholics who somehow managed to run a semi-profitable drug business out of their one room apartment. Casey was raised in large part by a grandmother so enamored with her Baptist religious beliefs and so sure of sex as the devil's primary exercise, she attempted to beat any sign of sexuality or gender out of her sole grandchild. The grandmother dressed Casey in boy's clothing and tried to pass her off in church as her sister's son. Casey didn't think many people believed her grandmother, and owing from the at first furtive, then open attempts by the boys in her Sunday school class to show her what a real boy looked like, she also thought her religious upbringing a sham, an ongoing joke expressly pulled on her.

When Casey's first period arrived, her grandmother made her sleep in the shed with a crusty blanket and a roll of paper towels. When the bleeding stopped and her cries of hunger increased (she was fed only burnt biscuits by her step-grandfather who leered at her naked body made even more sweaty as she tried to hide beneath the blanket; "Smells like sin in here, girl, and believe me, I know the smell of sin," he would say as she devoured the bread), her grandmother dragged the stained little girl to the house, tied her to the bedposts, and with the step-grandfather leaning in the doorway chewing a long stalk of grass, raped her repeatedly with a rolling pin until Casey passed out. The last thing she remembered her grandmother saying was how she had to teach Casey a lesson, "Lord knows."

+

The funeral ends, and although I am avoiding my mother's head as it swerves this way and that, I know she will see me when she leaves. As there is nowhere for me to go (the side door is blocked by cousins wearing black bands), I wait quietly in my pew until my mother is about to pass, her face red, eyes raw. She stretches her fingers toward me, and I take them and escort her out of the church, my stepfather's hand on my shoulder. On the church steps, my brother whispers with some relatives. Bagpipes compete with the traffic on the nearby boulevard. I just want to go home. While my parents are hugging distant relatives, I walk to the parking lot and leave.

Casey and I had a dog named F. Scott, but in a drunken rage after Casey died, I gave him to a friend of a friend who lives twenty miles to the north. I drive from Aunt Mel's funeral to his house but since I can't remember his name, I don't knock but instead peer over the gate whispering, "F. Scott? F. Scott?" There is no response and I drive home.

My apartment is down the block from the one Casey and I had. It is much larger and has what would be a writing room if I ever bothered to write again. On the way home, I had stopped at a liquor store and stocked up, but I didn't need to; after spending a morning amid the yellows of my parents' guest room, there is more than enough alcohol in my apartment. I pour myself a drink: a little tonic, a healthy knock of gin, two ice cubes, and stir. I will not go into the tub tonight, I tell myself. No sir, not tonight.

+

By the time Casey was thirteen, she had endured the rolling pin at least once every two weeks ("just so you don't forget"). The night her grandmother used a butter knife was the night Casey took to the streets.

Casey's physical development was rampant despite her grandmother's fervent efforts. But the jeers and jagged glances from the kids in school, the gobs of spit drooled on her cropped hair, the incessant theft of her textbooks (frequently found after classmates took turns urinating on them) reinforced her deviant upbringing. She was still dressed in boy's clothes. The young men in her class no longer pulled out their penises; instead, a cruel game emerged. The boys would try to corner her on the way to the girls' room or when she walked home (even at thirteen, Casey refused to run from her tormentors, choosing to uphold what little pride she may have had by the mere fact that she wouldn't alter pace). They would pin her down, and force their hands into her slacks. When two boys spent the length of a math class loudly sniffing their fingers, Casey was dismissed.

She remembered the trek home as her first taste of independence. Her grandmother would be at the church, tending to the small garden that stood just before the gravestones at the rear of the church property. Casey would have three full hours of freedom before the old woman's return. Her step-grandfather worked an odd shift; he would not arrive home until after Casey's seven o'clock bedtime. She recalled the smell of hyacinths drifting from the park, and despite the ache in her crotch from the morning's game, Casey discovered—for the first time—that there might be more to life than what she had known.

After spending a half hour running with the pre-schoolers (their mothers clutching at handbags whenever Casey squealed with joy), jumping from swing to sliding board to monkey bars in the forbidden playground ("a haven for winos and perverts just waiting to take what the Lord has given"), she hurried home and broke the lock on her grandparents' bedroom door. Casey would pause here in the telling and, after a long drag, say she knew then she was leaving or she would be dead, she was sure: sent home from school, breaking into the bedroom; Casey figured she had nothing left to lose. She pulled on her grandmother's pantyhose, smeared lipstick across her face, and then applied it as an eye shadow, trying to match the way her favorite teacher, Ms. Garrity, wore the pretty pale blue across her own lids. Ms. Garrity once gave Casey a flute, and for the duration of an afternoon, before her grandmother snapped it in two, the notes cascading into the wind were the most exquisite sounds Casey ever heard.

+

I sit in my stepfather's old chair and chain smoke cigarettes. I had given them up the last time Casey was in the hospital, but I started again after her funeral. I think I may have lit up during the service, but I'm not sure. A car slows down in front of my building (I'm on the first floor), and I run to the window to see if it's Eve, but I know it's not. Eve and I dated for four months about a year after Casey died. Everyone was real proud of me, my family, that is. "Time to move forward," they said, "nothing like time to heal old wounds, pal." Right.

+

When Casey heard the squeak of the mail truck, she checked herself in the only mirror in the house (hung inside her grandmother's closet beneath a contorted crucified Jesus glowing in the dark, His face flush and writhing), then took the stairs two at a time. Peeking behind the heavy curtains adorning the front windows, Casey could see the mail carrier, an unfortunate man named Leonard Licht, work his way slowly to her grandmother's house. Casey thought Leonard Licht handsome: his mustache neatly trimmed, the gray beneath his carrier cap shiny and combed back, a little mole on his left cheek that danced whenever his face twitched, which was quite often. Twice on different Saturdays, Casey greeted Leonard at the door only to be yanked back by her hair into the living room. "He's a drunkard, that one. Godless too," her grandmother would say, and Casey knew it was true; she had watched him sneak a silver flask from his mailbag when she spied on him from her bedroom window during her frequent lockdowns.

When Leonard Licht reached 114 Calvert Street, Casey swung the door open and propped herself against the flaking paint of the frame. Leonard tipped his cap and handed her the mail. "Can I have some?" Casey asked. After ascertaining the grandmother was at church and the old man at the mill, Leonard passed the silver flask, blocking her from view with his mailbag. "Don't tell the old lady," he said between gulps when she returned the liquor. The whiskey burned her throat; for a brief moment, she believed she would throw up on Leonard Licht's shoes. But after the initial nauseous wave, a feeling of immunity flowed through her blood. Squinting into the sun, she asked Leonard Licht if she could see his penis. Mr. Licht refused and backed off the porch. Undaunted, Casey pulled her grandmother's skirt up and wiggled the pantyhose down to her feet. "See, I don't have one." Casey told me that back then her crotch area was frequently scabbed. Leonard Licht took one look and high-tailed it back to his mail truck, his bag of letters left on the porch; he had taken the flask.

+

Eve was pretty in that cute way, too cuddly to be actually beautiful but nice to look at regardless. Eve cut hair and attended real estate school and didn't mind that I wandered from job to job and drank like they might stop making the stuff the day after tomorrow. She didn't mind either when, after we first tried to have sex, I broke down and spilled the Tale of Casey; Eve simply rocked me to sleep. Although she never mentioned the incident, the evening after I suggested she move in (a proposition I don't quite remember, having been halfway through a bottle of vodka), Eve asked if I was still in love with Casey. I lied. I was alone and scared and drinking my face off just about every night, so I lied. Eve moved in the next weekend; we had been a couple for a grand total of two months.

My sex drive remained strong, but I could not for the life of me maintain an erection. Eve wanted me to stop drinking or at least drink less so we could function and fuck like a normal couple, and I tried for a few weeks, but I could still not actively participate in intercourse. Eve seemed undaunted and determined to have me inside her, so she bought books, lots of books, some of which I still have. I found the authors' advice humorous to the extreme, and when Eve took to quoting passages between the sheets like twisted mantras, I fell off the bed. Eve was not amused. She started staying later at the library where she studied for her real estate license. Sometimes she wouldn't arrive back at the apartment until after nine o'clock.

One Monday night, Eve didn't come home at nine and still

wasn't back at eleven. By midnight, I had broken out the gin and was playing Doors records at maximum volume. At one in the morning, after my upstairs neighbor banged on his floor for the third time, I turned the Doors off and kneeled on the couch to better watch the street. I phoned Eve's best friend, a frightening redhead named Judy (but called Mimi by her close associates). Mimi cackled and said it was a poor excuse for a man who didn't know where his woman was laying her head at this late hour. I hung up on her and resumed my position on the couch, fortressed by an ever-decreasing bottle of gin. At three-thirty a car, not Eve's, pulled to the front of the apartment. I couldn't make out the driver, but it was a man. Eve stumbled up the drive and almost fell into me when I opened the door. She smelled of liquor, and her cheeks were crimson, her lips chapped.

"What the fuck are you looking at?"

Eve marched into the living room, made herself a fresh drink, and felt her way like a blind person to our bedroom.

"Fairy. Yeah, that's what you are. Hung up little faggot boy."

I said nothing.

"Fucking Casey. She's dead, and I can't get laid. Do you hear me faggot boy? She's dead and gone, and I can't get fucking laid."

My hands clenched and unclenched. I could say nothing.

"Why don't you just go to the cemetery and dig her up, huh? Why don't you just go and do that? Maybe you can join her. You'd like that. A razor should do the trick. No, wait. It's pills, isn't it?"

I jumped on her; I was hard and we had sex until she passed out. Eve packed her things and left in the morning. I repeated what I did when the friend of a friend came to pick up F. Scott; I walked to a bar four blocks away and stayed until I thought the deed was done.

+

Casey spent the rest of the October afternoon on the front porch, the pantyhose still around her ankles, reading other people's mail and daydreaming about what normal lives must be like: a letter from a brother, a note from a collection agency, a birthday card from someone's grandmother with a five dollar bill taped inside. She resealed the last, imagining what she would do with five dollars, pretending she was the recipient. The last piece of mail she read was a postcard of the New York City skyline from a Wanda Lopez to a Frank Williams. It hangs still, trapped beneath a Stones magnet on my refrigerator door. When her grandmother's car pulled into the driveway, Casey hid the postcard beneath the Jesus Loves You doormat, stood up, and vomited on the mailbag.

The rest of the day was a blur until the knife. The grandmother beat Casey with her purse, and once when they were inside the house, with a roll of quarters. Casey was tied naked to her bed and could hear her grandmother dialing the post office; the letter bag remained outside. The whole story unfolded on the phone ("help me, Lord", the old woman repeated) and was relayed to her husband still at work. An hour later, rope around her hands and feet, her mother's mom slid a butter knife into her vagina while her step-grandfather held her mouth shut with a hand smelling of Camel cigarettes. "This'll fix it, this will get the sex out of you now, girl," he said and smiled, a toothpick dancing between his chapped lips.

No doctor, no bandages, Casey remained bound to the bed well after dark, a washcloth shoved between her legs. She drifted in and out of consciousness. When she awoke in the night, her middle throbbing and her wrists chafed from the rope, she saw his shadow in the doorway, arms above his head, fingers splayed on the door frame. To Casey, it was Jesus come to administer the final punishment. She cried out to him, and the shadow became a man, a hand bearing a strong scent of Camels covered her mouth. "Shush now. Got to teach you something about it. Can't get pregnant now, girl, can you?" He forced himself into her, and she passed out.

When she awoke the next time, the ropes were off, and her grandmother's pantyhose were clumsily arranged around her waist. The way the sun had sneaked up on the horizon told her she had maybe a half hour before the old woman rose to make breakfast. Her bedroom door was unlocked.

She left with next to nothing, just a fresh pair of jeans slung over her shoulder and a box of tissues, pausing on the porch to take the postcard from beneath the doormat. Mr. Licht's bag was in the corner. Casey stood on the sidewalk before the house of her childhood in a stained t-shirt and her grandmother's pantyhose bulging with the dirty washcloth. She climbed back on the porch and dug through the mailbag, holding her nose. When she found the birthday card, she removed the five-dollar bill. Casey picked up a small black stone near the steps, wincing as she knelt, and scratched "I'm sorry, Happy Birthday, love Casey" below the nice grandmother's signature, and limped away.

+

My mother calls after I have achieved a steady level of inebriation.

"How are you?"

"I thought I heard Eve's car out front."

"Eve's gone, dear. Why don't you get some sleep?"

My mother is a very wise woman.

+

Casey's journey east ended in our little town of Rhawnhurst in Mondauk County. After months on the street, she relied on the kindness of a few distant aunts who shared a marked disdain for her maternal grandmother's faith. Casey wound her way from aunt to aunt until her parents' eventual sobriety and subsequent move back east.

Night after night, shot after shot, we recounted Casey's journey, the Tale of Casey, like a myth told generation to generation. We would walk F. Scott in the snow and try to piss our names in the slush. The stereo burst forth with the sounds of our parents' music, the sounds of the 60's; we reasoned it a better time with pinpoint focus in sharp relief to the blurs of our day. Our only fight revolved around a bright yellow shower curtain I claimed stung my eyes. We burned scented candles and spent hours in the bathtub, reading aloud, sometimes just sitting there, listening to the sound of the other's breath. We had sex but not often. Casey's past was an intimidation, but we never spoke of how it affected our bedroom activities. If the act went off without tears and didn't result in nightmares, we made silent thanks and went about our lives.

The night Casey resumed her self-mutilation, I was already liquored to the gills when she drew a bath. I declined on the grounds that if F. Scott couldn't join us, I didn't want to partake, which seemed to me a perfectly reasonable stipulation. Casey slid into the steamy water, and I tried to wash her back from a position on the side of the tub. When I almost slipped for the second time, Casey laughed and demanded that I bring her a fresh cocktail and then go to bed. I did as I was told and fell asleep in my damp clothes, the back scrubber still in my hand.

I awoke to Casey sitting on the edge of the bed, fiddling with an

Ace bandage. I asked her (through a thick layer of fuzz) what happened; she walked into the kitchen to make coffee. When I peed, I saw the blood on the inside of the tub. I said nothing. The cutting continued for the next month, never genuine suicide attempts, but each resulting in more Ace bandages, and still I said nothing. I stopped taking baths; I now took showers in record time. F. Scott started sleeping in the tub during the summer; it was cooler, and F. Scott didn't have to imagine Casey's pale blue eyes fixated on her carved skin, didn't have to imagine little Casey being forced to endure a rolling pin on a regular basis.

Casey was still in therapy then, and as the time between cuttings decreased, her therapist suggested it was time for an inpatient stay, the first in two years. I helped pack her bags and resolved to myself as I drove her to the hospital that I would stop drinking. I would be there for Casey when she was released. I even managed to convince myself to quit smoking. I kissed Casey good-bye in the waiting room as she was led away by the admitting nurse, telling her stupidly that I was just a phone call away. Casey smiled weakly and told me to go home and get some sleep. The smile said it all: you can't help, you couldn't even talk about it, there's nothing you can do. I resolved to change. I had found my purpose; Casey was my purpose.

+

F. Scott is in the backyard. It is past midnight, and the dog is still in the goddamn backyard. I climb the fence, and F. Scott growls once and licks my face with what I feel could only be waves of recognition. The gate is locked, and as I feed F. Scott some dog biscuits, I wonder how I will be able to lift him over the fence.

There is a shed on the opposite side of the in-ground pool. The doors are unlocked, and inside I find a pair of garden shears. I sit behind a rose bush and try to cut the fence. F. Scott curls up beside me. I wish I had brought something to drink; the few I had before the drive over were for courage, but now I need something to calm me down so I can think clearly.

The back porch light shimmers, and I see a figure in a robe. I lie still behind the rose bush. "F. Scott? Come on in, F. Scott." The dog's ears perk up, but instead of running inside, he barks and dances in a circle. "F. Scott? Come on, boy. F. Scott." There is a hitch in the voice, and the man in the robe descends to the backyard. "F. Scott.

What's wrong? You find a dead bird?" Pause. I can smell his aftershave. "What are you doing here? Are you okay?" I pull myself up and shake his hand; we both ignore the garden shears at my feet. It is the friend of a friend. "I'm okay. Came to see F. Scott." The dog sits between us, his head following the flow of words. "Do you want to come in? I could make some coffee or…" I shake my head with what I think is a fair share of regret. "Can't. Sorry. But thanks." The man tightens the belt around his robe. "Getting cold is what it is. Well, maybe next time, huh?" He glances at the gate. "Let me unlock that for you." He jogs into the house and returns with the key. We walk to my car, the passenger side parked on his lawn. "Nasty bit of weather lately. Bad for the rose bushes." We shake hands again, and he holds my car door open until I am safely inside. I can hear F. Scott barking over my Doors tape as I pull away.

+

My sobriety lasted a week after Casey's return, although I somehow refrained from smoking. Our lives resumed much in the same manner, with the exception that Casey dropped out of the current semester and was working almost full time at the little clothing store on the Avenue. Her therapy sessions were three times a week. I didn't try to have sex with her, and she never brought it up. Otherwise, all was normal. "No more cutting," she said, and I believed her. Casey wasn't drinking either, but after I commented on missing the sound of vodka being poured over ice, she walked to the cabinet where we used to keep the booze, found an airplane bottle behind some soup, and made me a salty dog. "It's okay. I can't for a while. Meds, you know," and she shook the little pill bottle. I nodded and drank the first of many.

As part of her homecoming celebration, I bought tickets to see Paul Simon. We marked the date on the calendar and practiced singing all the old Simon and Garfunkel songs; we wanted to be prepared. The night of the concert, Casey drove, and we played music trivia in the car. In the middle of the ride, Casey said, "I feel so old," and I said nothing. The show was exhilarating, a welcome respite from recent events, and on the way home, Casey suggested making a pitcher of iced tea and Southern Comfort. I grinned. "That's my girl." That's exactly what I said, just like that: "That's my girl."

We finished the pitcher and started doing shots of Comfort, Janis blasting in the background. Casey called for a bath, and I deferred to her better judgment, partially disrobing in the kitchen. "Someone's excited," she said, looking down. I kissed her neck, but she didn't smell like Casey, and I stopped. We did another shot. Casey lit a cigarette and led me into our little bathroom. I couldn't see for the alcohol, but I could hear the bath water, the distant thunder drums of the tub being filled. I stumbled back into the bedroom. All I could picture was skin beaten so severely, blood bounced into the air. I felt sick. "Oh, I have to lie down." And not for the first time, I passed out, half-clothed, upon the bed. All that was missing was the back scrubber.

+

It is time. I light the candles and my glass jingles with the sound of ice about to expire. The tub is sparkling clean; I scrubbed it down like a surgeon not an hour ago, not two gin and tonics ago. The water splashes into the tub, and the drum-like sound it makes should sound familiar but does not.

+

She floated.

Casey was dead at least three hours before I awoke. All the medication she swallowed must have made her buoyant. The yellow shower curtain shielded her eyes from mine. I remember yelling into the telephone. I wanted to reach out and bring her close to my face, perform mouth to mouth, cover her body so no one else would see her naked. I did nothing. She floated. I remember a friend walking F. Scott. The dog startled me awake with his crying and whining. F. Scott's black fur was wet and slick near his face. I remember the glare of the ambulance and the way the alcoholic who lived next to us nervously peered through his front door as the emergency technicians rushed into our apartment. I remember wanting to hold her one last night and smell her skin. I did nothing. She floated. I recall very little of my shoving match with the cop, of him asking me what type of recreational drugs we took the night before, of me trying to explain about the rolling pin, about the swing set and the postcard. And all the while, Casey floated.

+

The first time, I must admit, I was scared I would fall asleep, and then, without notice, that became the game.

I wonder if the little black baby who was fed too much oxygen by Aunt Mel found it easier to float; I wonder: if your insides are filled with too much of anything, if that's all you know how to do in the end: float.

My mother calls just before I go to sleep. She wants me to know how much she and my stepfather love me. I want to say "I love you" back, but I don't. The words are like a stone holding down my tongue. I say nothing.

+

I was without purpose.

The little girl with golden curls was Casey's much younger half sister, and I remember weaving up the aisle toward the vestibule after her and someone, my stepfather maybe, forcing me back into a pew. Everything smelled like candles, and I wanted to vomit on my shoes. The candles masked the smell of Casey. My parents' anchored me. My grandmother and Aunt Mel passed me hard candies for reasons I didn't quite understand. When the priest hit the part about ashes to ashes, dust to dust, I started to laugh and could not make myself stop.

I wondered what F. Scott was doing; I hoped he wasn't lying in the tub. It was October and still warm. F. Scott wouldn't stop crying; he had smelled death and had tried to rescue Casey. I have to get rid of the dog if only for his own good. He has to let go.

+

If I lower my head, I hear the whole world. A few times I think I hear F. Scott, but he lives with the friend of a friend. Submerged, the little hairs on my arms dance and stretch out, luxuriant in their freedom. I don't feel sleepy, but if I do, well, ashes to ashes and not enough oxygen. Every morning arrives, and I am shivering in my wrinkled skin. It's a rite of passage, every night. I can sleep nowhere else now. I do this religiously; I have to maintain my purpose. If I lower my head, I hear the whole world. I am floating.

I hear my own heart beating and wonder when it will stop.

-end-

Stories of Zen and Want

upon a sculpture, green and small

"nobody, not even the rain, has such small hands"
E. E. Cummings, "somewhere i have never
traveled, gladly beyond"

Recommended Soundtrack:

"Between The Bars" by Elliot Smith

"I Love You" by Sarah McLachlan

"Gorecki" by Lamb

1

submerged
i await you;
your fingers: delicate, discrete,
discover notes among
hardened lines and force
to my parched throat songs
long buried—

emerged
i am without name;
your eyelids flutter
and the sinews
of your fingers bind us;
conceived, punished into your distant image,
i am willed to song—

adorned
i am without purpose;
upon the shelf, i can be near
you but your fingers
no longer seek me out;
my song dies upon your
lips the moment they thought to touch—

2

"hey bartender,
my throat is like that which is barren…"

i lean forward to hear
secret whisperings among the smoldered ends
and smudged reflections—

"hey bartender,
my tongue tastes like that of ashes…"

the sculpture is between my fingers,
vulgar in beauty, twisted in motion,
whole but not filled—

"hey bartender,
my soul is like that of the glass before me…"

i peer in and stare back—

"hey bartender,
i am like the circle incomplete…"

the stool adjacent spins quietly;
among concaves of watermarks,
i await you—

3

i need to feel your mind

when our shoulders touched,
i could smell the wood chips in your hair,
and when you placed the sculpture in my hand,
like a conduit of wine, it filled me, and
my fingers composed between the wild lines
of your palm thoughts into scribble—

i need to feel your mind:
versace gilded, country heather tinged,
untamed appetite,
enchantress—

the symbols overflow
onto paper white and joust for position;
i am barren and stained now: the syllables
have all been arranged—

the sculpture is before me and i await you

Shoes Hanging

"Freedom's just another word for nothing left to lose."
Janis Joplin, "Me and Bobby McGee"

Recommended Soundtrack:

"Me And Bobby McGee" {acoustic demo version}
by Janis Joplin

"Your Song" by Elton John

"Superstar" by Sonic Youth

"My Favorite Things" {from *The Sound of Music*}
by Julie Andrews

"Somewhere" by Tom Waits

So someone touched the edge of her blanket and walked again. But I'm getting ahead of myself. It all began with a dare, really. Her brother threw Woofer out the car window, and I surrendered to her dare. Now she's Saint Abigail of Rhawnhurst or some such shit.

Across the street, sitting on a curb, I close my eyes, and their voices sound like the noise you get when you run through the radio dials:

-Doesn't she look pretty today, Madge?

-I hope the line isn't long this morning. I have to take the baby to the Avenue for her checkup.

-It's all bullshit, I tell you.

-Then why are you here, sir? Just go home.

-Yesterday, the baby and me had to wait almost two hours, and then it started to rain, really pour.

-It's all bullshit, I tell you.

-Yes, she does. Do you remember when Aunt Aggie was laid out? Now there was a work of art, I tell you.

Her parents make them form a line down the edge of the street so their blankets and picnic baskets won't block the sidewalk. They shuffle in a crooked line and lean on the parked cars. Mr. Menkee comes out of his house each morning and pretends to wash his car so that maybe they won't rest on his Chevrolet. Our neighborhood used to be filled with the noises of every neighborhood around here: playing cards in bicycle spokes, the cry of safety during a late game of freeze-tag, someone's dog chasing a stray hockey ball as it rolled toward the sewer. Now the faithful bring their own brand of clamor, and the kids who live here mostly sit on their moms' porches, sucking store-bought popsicles while watching the daily parade. Even the ice cream man doesn't drive down our block anymore, although Jimmy Festeri told me he once saw the driver waiting in line.

Ours was the kind of neighborhood that used to work best as a single organism. It was our little network of streets that kept the produce man alive, my mother swore. His rickety truck would burst into view, and the loudspeaker atop would herald, "Strawberries, strawberries! Three boxes for a dollar! Strawberries!" While the rest of the world embraced all-night convenience stores and giant supermarkets, we gorged ourselves on the produce man's farm-fresh offerings.

Last summer's Little Eddie Onion incident is the best tale of our collective triumph. We were playing wire ball, and an odd bounce saw the green tennis ball accelerating down the street—the mouth of the sewer waiting in salivating hunger (or so Eddie would describe). Little Eddie Onion, third son of Art and Mary Runyon (he of little league coaching fame and she the winner of the church Bundt cake bake-off), being the last of three brothers and therefore not one to wait for things to happen, took chase while we rested on the Russians' front lawn. Abigail was there of course; she had burned a few berries she'd picked behind the Menkees' garage, between the fences, and had painted her face with war-like blueberry streaks. Disturbingly, her dimples were filled in with the same color so when she smiled (and every single boy on the street blushed to his toes), her dimples rose like little stars and danced before returning to hibernation. We all wanted to kiss her, but no one even tried. Abigail ruled over the neighborhood with little effort; the sheer amount of early adolescent love was an invisible crown. She was our referee, judge, peacemaker, war chief, and gang leader. In all things, Abigail was consulted first. Even the older kids often followed her word, never passed lightly, to the letter. We loved her and she allowed herself to be loved.

Little Eddie Onion hit the patch of leaves and moist dirt near the sewer, fell on his back, and slid down into its mouth. The sewers on our streets did not have grates; rather, the openings were built into the curbs and the manholes into the pavement above. The drop was some ten feet. Abigail was halfway to the sewer before we realized Little Eddie Onion was screaming for help. He landed in a cushiony mixture of sewage and foliage. Jimmy Festeri said he landed in shit.

"Eddie, breathe through your mouth," said Abigail, "I'll be down in a second."

We knocked on doors and alerted adults. Mr. Jukes used the handle of a shovel to pry the manhole cover open, but it was Abigail who was lowered to reach Little Eddie Onion.

"No one else will fit," said Abigail, "and, besides, I know how to breathe through my mouth."

Abigail was wearing a light skirt that afternoon, and she simply let down the zipper and stepped out of it. Mr. Runyon and Mr. Jukes lowered Abigail by her ankles (each boy pretending to not look at her muscular thighs or little white underwear), and she hoisted Little Eddie Onion by his wrists to safety. Jimmy Festeri was right: Eddie was covered in shit. He would not let go of Abigail's leg. I can say without hesitation, every boy on the block would surely have slept in poop to have his face against Abigail's thigh. The police were there a minute or two after the rescue, and they had to part the swelling of the neighborhood so the emergency team could inspect Little Eddie Onion. An impromptu block party ensued, and the adults devised schemes to block the sewer openings. The children gathered behind the Runyons' garage, and Abigail and Eddie retold their tale. We listened, enraptured. Abigail had never put her skirt back on.

I am no better than the ladies with the blue hair and rosary beads. I come to see Abigail every day. I don't try to speak to her parents anymore. The last time I attempted to explain myself, Abigail's mother started to hum a church hymn ("Faith of Our Fathers," I think), and her dad turned up the ball game on television. Her parents didn't know what else to do. They went about the business of living without a single ounce of outside stimuli affecting their behavior. Only when I tried to explain to her parents, in the wake of Abigail's Fall, what we were doing in the forbidden tree in the first place did they react somewhat normally: her mother slapped my face, and then both parents hugged me until I thought I would be crushed. I didn't allow myself to cry in front of her folks or in front of my own; I saved my tears for the lonely moment every night when I switched off the bedside lamp and tried to see past the darkness, the outline of the tree burning behind wet eyelids.

-*I could not see and now I have sight!*

-*And what is wrong with you?*

-*You must have faith—there is no other way.*

-*Shhh. It's the AIDS.*

-*Okay, people? If we could all just come back to the church basement, I'm sure that Mrs. Paul has the coffee on.*

-*I'm alright, mister. I'm not going to be six.*

-*It's not magic; without faith, you can touch her blanket all day.*

-*We can talk about this and pray together. Surely God has not intended for us to worship this poor girl in her garage.*

-*Ah, Father. That's the problem with the Church. They can't see the miracles that are happening in their own backyard.*

-*Why don't you move her up in line? Here, take my place.*

Abigail was the only girl I ever willingly kissed, and I only kissed her once, although I had been dreaming about it since the day we met. Abigail moved to the neighborhood, right next door, when I was in the second grade; she became my best friend. As we progressed through the grades, I developed a crush on Abigail. She was only slightly shorter than I was, with muscular arms and a quick laugh that lit her overly large eyes like pinball lights. Her dirty blonde hair always smelled like bark. I even peeked through my windows to catch her undressing; her room was across the shared driveway from mine. Alas, it is to my deepest regret that nothing more than the brightness of her thighs was ever visible to me. I never told anyone how I would lie in bed and pretend Abigail was asleep on my chest, although we hadn't slept in the same bed since the fifth grade. I was afraid my love would invalidate the friendship, as though anything could.

Abigail, with the same wisdom she used to rule the neighborhood, never acknowledged the crush directly. Instead, the Queen of Rhawnhurst began a campaign to wean me from the night sweats. As far as I could tell, and I never actually asked her, the war she waged seemed entirely dependent upon gas. That is, Abigail would fart as much as possible around me. Knowing Abigail, I can only imagine her diet was curtailed to this single purpose, for she was nothing if not succinct and direct. The initial farts, managed or not, I discreetly ignored, as much as a grade-schooler could. Abigail would lift her skirt, scrunch her face, and release a rather noisy emission. After several weeks of pretending my best friend wasn't ripping them on a regular basis, I borrowed money from my mother and bought Abigail a set of candles. I wrapped them like a birthday present. Abigail opened the package and, with her dimples at full attention, lit a candle, dropped her shorts, and blew out the flame with a well-aimed fart. And although we rolled around, choked with laughter, nothing could deter the love that made it hard to go to sleep at night.

-*What would everyone think if I suggested that we leave now and head straight to the church?*

-*I made eggs.*

-*It's all bullshit, I tell you.*

-*Father, what harm are we doing?*

-*I heard that where she fell, roses grew.*

-*Frank, don't you think her parents have suffered enough?*

-*No, no, not roses—lilies. Someone my sister goes to school with was there and saw 'em.*

-*Then why are you here? Why don't you just leave and let someone who believes take your place in line?*

-*Lilies? Didn't she fall by the church?*

-Thou shalt worship one God.

-Her backyard. She fell in her backyard.

-I heard it was off a bridge, and when she hit the water, it turned crystal clear and all the frogs started singing.

Abigail had a brother named Mark Thomas, and Mark Thomas hated Abigail. It seems to me now that the motivation was jealousy, pure and simple (as if anything could be). Mark Thomas was awkward and deceitful, whereas Abigail acted with grace and absolute sincerity. Mark Thomas, or Markie as his parents called him, suffered from severe acne that seemed to emerge from his back, from beneath his t-shirt collar, and swarm his face like an invading army. Abigail had clear pale skin. Markie was always in the back of the picture, just behind the action. During lengthy bouts of freeze-tag or freedom, Markie was there, although he did not participate. Covered in dirt, his hair matted with mud, his face streaked with what I assumed were tears, Mark Thomas would sit behind the bush on the Menkees' lawn and watch until his mother called out for supper.

Both siblings were obsessed with art; their mother was a painter of some renown (that is, her work hung in a few local offices, including our grade school principal's), and their father taught art history and drawing at the local preparatory school. It was Abigail's art contest, of all things, that led to her beatification. Abigail frequently organized the neighborhood children's activities, corralling them to act out the rumble scene from *West Side Story* in the backyard, bang percussion in a band, or collect old teddy bears for the Boys' Home on Castor Avenue. On the last Saturday of every month, Saint Abigail would spread her collection of Mary, Mother of God, statues on the front lawn for a good cleaning. The younger kids would assist, and Mr. Jukes would sometimes cook vegetables on the grill for us when we were finished—it was quite an array of holy figures and the cleaning ate up the afternoon. We took to calling that last Saturday "Marys on the Lawn Day." After refusing to audition for an upcoming Abigail production, I was handed a legal pad and some pens. Abigail told me that if I turned her down as an actor, then I would have to be the playwright, a task I embraced after much procrastination. Today I still write long hand on yellow legal pads.

It was the Time of the Contests. The art competition, "Up Your Art," was Abigail's latest venture, and fliers detailing the guidelines soon papered every tree and telephone pole. The kids who couldn't draw were drafted as judges, along with the widow Mrs. Bates who, although blind in one eye and with only a measuring of sight in the other, once painted a rather serene picnic scene on the wooden fence surrounding her backyard. The prize: an old pair of Abigail's roller skates, hand decorated in magic marker by the benefactress herself.

Abigail was the only kid on the block to call Mrs. Bates by her first name, Sara, and she spent many an evening reading philosophical texts and *Lives of the Saints* aloud to her after giving us last minute instructions for the night's activities. Freedom was Abigail's favorite game, and it was Mrs. Bates who told her, "You have to rid yourself of everything to be really free." To us, Mrs. Bates was a funny old lady who would nod her head toward Abigail and repeat, every time she saw her it seemed, "Doesn't she have a wonderful figure?" To our future saint, Sara Bates was a touchstone—a vision of where she saw herself in sixty years.

On the morning of the contest, the air was dense with last minute scribbling. Summer was nearing its close and the glare of the sun on the parked cars covered Abigail's porch in jagged spotlights. I remember leaning against the tree in front of her house and watching her direct the little ones, each wearing a paper badge labeled "Art Assistant," hanging the finest that Stanwood Street offered with colored thumb tacks. Judgment time was set for noon, and two little girls in identical halter-tops and shorts were sent across the street to escort the limping Mrs. Bates. A record player was dragged to the porch, and Abigail instructed Little Eddie Onion to play "Ode to Joy" over and over followed (after the declaration of the winner) by "We Are the Champions." The roller skates were on a small table; picked flowers, pixie sticks, and string cheese sprouted from beneath dirty laces tied into a bow.

First, second, and third place winners were chosen after a lengthy delay. (Mrs. Bates dropped her glasses into one of the roller skates while attempting to sneak off with some of the string cheese.) Fuller Street Agnes was declared the winner; Cory Gazer placed second; Highland Avenue Agnes took third. The Saturday afternoon air was warm, and the adults were milling around, hands clasped behind their backs, admiring each picture as Abigail acted as tour guide. No one noticed Mark Thomas at first; he stood in the driveway near the side of the porch, breathless, clutching an oversized sketch pad drawing of his and Abigail's stuffed animals, aligned as if they were sitting for a family portrait. His face was wet and circles were around his eyes. Abigail pulled him aside and told him the contest was over. Some of the older kids laughed. Mark Thomas ripped his drawing in half and pushed past Abigail, running to the corner and disappearing.

As we discovered later inside the garage, the stuffed animals were posed leaning against the family station wagon. Mrs. Bates wagged her head and exited, string cheese stuffed into her sleeves alongside her tissue reserve. Front and center was Woofer, Abigail's almost constant companion. Abigail's parents had won Woofer at a local church carnival when Abigail was six (a few short weeks before she'd moved across from my window). I suppose the stuffed dog's original guise was Sherlock Holmes, but it was hard to see that now. Woofer looked like he'd been through the mill—his stuffing was outside as well as in, both of his eyes were gone, and where his Holmesian pipe once protruded, there flapped an unhealthy looking, faded lavender tongue. Abigail loved Woofer unconditionally, and most times the dog could be found a few feet away from the scene, propped up against the wheel of a bicycle or placed atop a neighbor's shrub. If the time before Woofer's untimely departure was the Time of the Contests, then in his wake we entered the Time of the Dares. But I'm ahead of myself.

With "Up Your Art" winding down, Abigail tugged at my sleeve, and we hopped backyard fences, through our hiding place behind the Menkees' garage, until we were on the other side of Solly Avenue where the woods ran up to the edge of the street. This was traditional behavior; Abigail liked to escape with me after major neighborhood events and relive their glory or tragedy while we walked along the edge of the woods, looking for wild berries. It was there we first noticed the shoes hanging—the shadows of the sneakers dangling from the high wire blocked the sinking of the sun.

"I like the way they look."

"First words I ever said, according to my father."

Converse, Keds, jogging shoes.

" 'Shoes hanging.' "

Abigail's story was as familiar to me as Woofer's torn exterior was to her.

"My dad was driving down the street…"

Pumas, tennis shoes, high tops.

"…and I wasn't even two…just a little girl…"

Dress shoes, boondockers, an old pair of work boots.

"…I looked up and pointed and said it…"

Spikes, moccasins, but mostly sneakers. Lots of sneakers.

"...'shoes hanging.'"

"Why do they do that?" I asked, looking furtively around as if, at any moment, a gang of sneaker-wielding brigands would launch their footwear airborne toward the late summer sky.

Abigail knew the answer, of course. In all things, even in her most tragic of times, the truth never hid from Abigail. As I write this, my chest swells, and deep inside my brain, I can smell the bark in her hair.

"Ritual, I guess. It's the way each person approaches the wire."

It was then I kissed her. It was under the shoes hanging from a wire on the outskirts of our world, Abigail's world, the neighborhood, that my lips, trembling, brushed and held hers, soft and steady.

Brushed, held, and released.

My rib cage barely contained the rapid beats, and my corduroys felt tight about the waist. The last rays of the sun caught her cheekbones, and with the camera I borrowed from my mother for the art show, I took Abigail's photograph, her dirty blonde hair tossed about her head, her eyes mad with mischief, her lips swollen (I believed) from their most recent dalliance with my own.

"I think they make a wish and then throw them."

Abigail closed in on me, her breath Juicy Fruit fresh, the soft down of her cheeks like snow.

"Make a wish," she said.

And then she kissed me. Again.

Brushed, held, released.

To this day, it is the single greatest moment of my life. I have no idea why she kissed me except that maybe Abigail was moved by the slight shiver of fall in the air. Perhaps she was curious or felt sorry for me—a mercy kiss—saddled as I was with unrequited love. But I like to think it was the coming autumn. She felt its chill on the back of her neck and in the pit of her stomach—Abigail always hated October—and sought warmth from the one friend who knew the subtleties between adoration and worship. The photograph sits now on my night table, and sometimes, late at night, I roll back my left sleeve and gently cover my upper arm with kisses meant for Saint Abigail. But I'm way ahead of myself. Again.

Abigail's parents kept a place at the Jersey shore, and frequently I would be invited, squished in the back of their station wagon with suitcases, picnic baskets, stuffed animals, and a glowering, acne-scarred Mark Thomas. It was during one of these jaunts to a weekend at the shore that Woofer's life (and all of ours I guess) took an unexpected turn.

-It was touching her blanket that did it.

-Whatever it was, my daughter walks now, and walking is good enough for me, no matter what Father says.

-Bullshit, bullshit, bullshit.

-God loves her, and that's all that counts.

-We love her, and that's all that counts.

-Poor Markie. Lad never had much going for him, did he?

-Did you see the holy cards the children made?

-Saint Abigail, my ass. Wait til Father Hoskins sees this.

-It was the old woman. Taught her everything.

-Think it might rain? Someone told me they wheel her in if it rains.

-Blanket doesn't work in the rain, is what I heard.

Mark Thomas had a mean streak, but Abigail was quicker. Rather than focus on his estimable artistic skills, Markie fixated on his sister with a determination usually held by a hunter for his game. Again and again, I would warn Abigail not to bite, not to react or return the volley, for that was her brother's goal. But Abigail, for all her intelligence, could not resist attacking back.

"I saw you two."

It was Mark Thomas above the din of the expressway, above the passage of tinny AM radio pop songs floating in the hot stale air of his parents' station wagon. I remember the soundtrack to our tragedy's automobile prologue: the Carpenters' "Superstar," Elton John's "Your Song," Johnny Nash singing "I Can See Clearly Now"—remember? "Jean" by Oliver, "Spinning Wheel" by Blood, Sweat, and Tears, Creedence telling us about the boys "Down on the Corner"—remember those? I can never forget; they are ingrained in my blood, spinning still.

I was in the middle, trying to ignore him. Abigail pushed her face dangerously close to mine.

"What did the crater say?"

"I said I saw you two. After the contest."

I could see their mother's left ear turning toward the conversation ever so slightly.

"You can see over those bumps, Markie? Goodie for you."

Abigail's face brushed mine and her hand played along the hem of my shorts.

"I saw you on Solly Avenue."

My heart doubled, and suddenly the whooshing air in the station wagon was bereft of oxygen. Abigail's mother leaned back in her seat.

"I saw you two kissing."

Abigail's mother tuned her tightly coifed head toward ours. My face was a lighthouse beacon of red. Abigail never flinched.

"We saw you sword fighting with Little Eddie Onion in the back of the Runyons' garage," said Abigail.

Mark Thomas' cheeks sunk into a giant "O," and all semblance of color leaked from his face into two shiny crimson fists. The reference was clearly over their mother's head. She turned back to stare out the bug besotted dashboard window.

It was true. A few weeks before, while sneaking down the narrow alleyway separating the Runyons' garage from old man Kensey's, we could hear soft murmuring from inside one of them. Abigail placed her ears against the peeling white paint flecks decorating the outside of the Runyons' garage. I was nervously pulling at a patch of crab grass. The murmuring turned to giggles and sounds of challenge pierced the air.

"It's Markie."

"Leave him be. You promised."

What I thought Abigail had promised was that she would watch me pee, an event that caused no amount of sleep to disturb the rigidity of my body all through the previous night.

"Lift me up."

"Abigail…"

"Give me a boost."

With a due amount of reluctance, I laced my hands together and Abigail used them as a stepping stool to peer past the dust encrusted side window. The pure white snow of the underside of Abigail's thigh pressed against my nose. I thought I might die from wanting.

"Jesus Christ!"

"What is it?"

"Jesus, Mary, and Joseph!"

We switched places, and there was Mark Thomas, naked except for his socks, battling it out like Errol Flynn with an equally bare-assed Little Eddie Onion, their short swords at attention, whacking and rubbing against the other's.

"Now that's something you don't see every day."

Those were Abigail's final words on the subject, despite repeated confused queries from me, and I finally released my bladder safe inside my house, Mark Thomas' display having eclipsed any planned event of my own.

Back in the station wagon, I leaned closer to Abigail and kept my eye on Markie's trembling mass of fists. His temper was renowned, and surely I would be the recipient of not a few of his flurries. Abigail remained unmoved.

"There better not be any kissing going on, I can tell you that much."

Abigail's mother's sidelong glance to her father told me that perhaps my Johnny-Carson-watching sleepovers were coming to a swift end, a situation already predicted by my conservative mother not a week before.

Without much effort, Abigail deflated the situation.

"Eww. Boys."

Mark Thomas' predicted reign of knuckles never launched, and not until after a quick bathroom break half-way to Jersey did any sign of his revenge become apparent, and by then, it was too late, too late for all of us, although we didn't know it.

"Shit. Where's Woofer?"

"Young lady, the language!"

Abigail and I began a frantic search throughout the seats and what we referred to as the back-back of the station wagon. The Sherlock Holmes of stuffed dogs appeared to be caught within a mystery of his own.

As we pulled away: "Perhaps you left him at home."

That was her mother's sole advice, but Woofer being detained at the homestead while we traveled to the Jersey shore was no more likely than Abigail having some naked sword fight with me.

Mark Thomas sneered, and that's when I saw Woofer's ear, or part of it, sticking out from beneath the right passenger side door. Abigail's eyes widened. I rolled the window down, and we both stuck out our heads. There was Woofer, smacking along the expressway. Somehow, while we climbed back into the station wagon the "cool way," via the back-back, Mark Thomas had managed to close our door so that the poor dog dangled from his right ear.

Abigail tapped my leg and held my hand. Not a sound did she make, but her eyes remained wide in a permanent stare, her head thrust out the window, watching what surely was the roughest ride of Woofer's existence, and this from a dog who fell out of trees, got buried in backyard treasure hunts, and floated with his owner during pool parties. Mark Thomas' face qualified every inch of his defeat. Abigail did not tell on him nor did she beseech her father to stop the car. It wasn't until we reached a stop light at the end of our exit, did she ease the door open and retrieve the battered Woofer, now significantly thinner, as a fair portion of his insides decorated the expressway between Pennsylvania and New Jersey.

Our brief vacation dragged in light of the tragedy, but Abigail refused to give Mark Thomas the satisfaction of even acknowledging her pain, thus enraging her brother to the point of a new dangerous-looking acne eruption. As soon as Markie left the room or the beach, Abigail's face sunk; even my entreaties to endure her flatulence raised only a distant smirk. But she allowed nothing to Mark Thomas except perhaps an extra helping of kindness, including him, to my chagrin, in our castle building and wave gliding, events Markie usually watched from afar.

But the final blow was to be Mark Thomas'; Abigail could not dampen his embarrassment with a soft hand and a stoic face. The ride home proceeded in a rather normal, sleepy, post-vacation malaise. We were in the middle of another tired verse of "Ninety-Nine Bottles of Beer on the Wall" when Markie snatched Woofer from between Abigail's sunburned muscular arms and released him out the open window onto the expressway. Woofer was gone.

Abigail reached over me and grabbed Mark Thomas by the balls, clenching her pretty little hand into a twisted vice grip. Markie sunk into his seat, his countenance a ghost face. Even the hairs on his head and the pimples on the back of his neck seemed to stand at strict attention. After a few minutes passed, Abigail released and started singing, effectively covering up her brother's loud sucking gasps and his eventual vomiting out the window. All this passed without a single nod from either parent; both were humming along to the sounds of AM radio's hot hits of summer.

With the car unpacked and Mark Thomas wisely completing his transition into a ghost, Abigail grabbed my hand and we sneaked down the street, around the corner, and stood beneath the forbidden tree just outside of the spiked church house fence. The tree was a monster: timeless and gnarled and bitter. Abigail's father said the Sycamore was quite dead and therefore even more dangerous; we were sworn to never climb the tree, a promise my fear of heights made quite unnecessary. Not even the battalion of squirrels who frequently raided our streets bothered with it much. To the children in the neighborhood, the tree was mythical and whether or not it was the oldest and tallest of all the trees lining our insignificant side streets mattered little—it loomed large in our minds. We called it the Hanging Tree. From its achingly long branches, an end-of-his-tether drinker, a retired Air Force mechanic, pitched himself into hell. Or so it was said.

Soft light from the street lamp a block down and muted colors from the church cast winsome shadows out of the clutches of the tree, and the telephone and electrical wires strewn across the sky were thrown into bold relief. Abigail just stood beneath them, staring up, her fists opening and closing, biting her lips. I shivered in the breeze; autumn was sneaking a finger into the night air. Abigail knocked her sneakers off and took them into her hands without breaking her gaze from the wires.

"Fuck him."

I slid my sneaks off too.

"Fuck him fuck him fuck him," she said.

Following Abigail's lead, I tied the individual laces into an impenetrable knot.

"Woofer."

Abigail's eyes never wavered from the wire as her sneakers deftly left her shaking hands, somersaulted, and twirled themselves magnificently around the wire.

"Shoes hanging."

My sneakers entered the brisk night and tore back down to the top of my head. There was no laughter. Several attempts later (one involving the trunk of a nearby parked car), Abigail gently removed the sneakers from my hand and hurled them into the sky.

"Make a wish."

The barefoot walk home was silent, and as I lay in bed, the shade bent so enough street light danced on Abigail's photograph, I honed my wish against the friendship until nothing was left but blunt desire and a coppery bottomless guilt. Abigail's window remained dark throughout the night. A block and a half away, my sneakers hung next to Abigail's, and I guessed the phone reception on Hasbrook Avenue suffered a noticeable bump in service.

Thus began the Time of the Dares.

-And there's the rub. The Church has to sanction this? You know how long Scottie's suffered from allergies? Christ.

-Are they really going to cut the blanket up and sell off little pieces?

-I don't see how the envelopes we fill each week have helped any of us.

And they continued to come, lining the curb, sleeping in cars, ordering pizza from Angelo's.

-What I don't understand is why her?

-She was an angel, that one.

-She was a troublemaker, pure and simple.

-An angel, I tell you.

-My daughter has a photograph of her hanging in her closet. Strangest thing but she said it makes her feel safe.

-The thing with the girls? Please. That mess was no saint.

And they spread the Word and news stations arrived and left with footage of our sad little circus.

-Then why are you here?

-Go home then.

-The thing is, ladies, the thing is—you just don't know. You just don't know. Redemption could be just around the corner.

The Time of the Dares got a running start the next day after Abigail and I walked to the Avenue and bought matching black Chucks, normally a summer commencement event fraught with the tingle only the looming last of day of school provided. This day brought a different sensation, and as I struggled to keep pace with Abigail, I knew the end of summer would prove to be as gray and sinister as it felt.

I had spent the morning counting my change, arranging silver coins and pennies into towering stacks. The Five and Dime sold stuffed animals, and I came to the financial conclusion that if I mowed a few lawns in the next day or so and then again before summer's end, I could afford to buy Abigail a new stuffed animal friend. We had three weeks before school began; that was my cutoff.

The transition of the neighborhood from art gallery and musical stage to the Time of the Dares was simple and swift. Within days, I was grounded an entire weekend for egging both the Ukrainians' house and Mr. Jukes' Volkswagen with Al Bossi (we also soaped our own houses to distance ourselves from the reign of eggs); Fuller Street Agnes, Jenny, and Little Kathie mimed "The Boogie Woogie Bugle Boy of Company B" in the raw; and Little Eddie Onion gave himself a tattoo of a basketball using a cigarette lighter, a bent paper clip, and a Paper Mate. In the middle of the unstringing of our neighborhood stood Abigail, her dirty blonde hair pushed atop her forehead in an act of intense concentration, her brother lurking just behind the next garbage pail. The only time normalcy prevailed was when Abigail would cease scheming to read to the widow Mrs. Sara Bates.

Nothing was sacred, and Abigail spared little in her wake. Early morning boners were revealed and inspected and discussed and pinged upon by skinny girls' fingers; the steps of the church became a blackboard, with magnified genitalia chalked in pink and orange; parents' night tables were raided for money, pornographic materials, sexy underwear; pets suddenly found themselves in frequent organized races between old police barriers in the fields bordering the train tracks and the woods.

"Let go of everything," Abigail said.

"Let go of everything."

Spin the Bottle and its more sinister cousin, Seven Minutes in Heaven, became primary conduits for Abigail's new spin on our waning summer. Games were arranged in basements (especially Stephanie Regan's), sheds, under porches, and frequently in Little Eddie Onion's ramshackle garage. It was there, amid rusted bicycles and deflated footballs, that Abigail first kissed a girl: Debbie Kay from over on Craig Street. The bottle spun on its lazy axis, and Debbie found herself, not for the first time, with the open end facing another girl—this time the Dark Lord Abigail. Debbie was loud; she wore grownup makeup and tight purple shorts that made every boy on the block groan when she walked by or sunbathed with Little Eddie Onion's older sister. Al Bossi and Chris Lee once purposely spilled a Slurpee cup of pennies in Debbie's presence just to watch her bend over to help in the retrieval process.

"Shit. Spin again."

Abigail deftly spit behind her, and her voice swam in the Runyon's house-of-cards garage.

"No. If Debbie wants to be in, then she has to play by the rules. No safety."

Debbie Kay launched herself onto her haunches; I could hear Joey Runyon catch his breath as her thighs strained against the famous purple shorts.

"No way."

Abigail pushed the bottle from the center of our tight circle.

"Then you leave."

"I'll leave."

"Then you can't come back."

"Fine."

"Then everyone here, everyone, will tell in school that you did anyway. Stay and it stays here."

Nobody moved, and it seemed as if the musty smell of abandoned toys and beyond-repair lawn mowers crept closer and closer, stuffing our noses with the smell of things in a permanent state of change and decay.

"No tongue."

"My way or the highway, babe."

Abigail sprung from her place and pulled Debbie and her purple shorts from the garage floor. Their embrace lasted, per Abigail's strict established rules, one minute. Jimmy Festeri kept time on his digital watch. Seven mouths held their breaths and released as Abigail backed away and pushed Debbie Kay out of the circle.

"Oh Christ."

"Agnes, shhh."

"It's not right."

Abigail pulled herself to her full height and spun a cool circle on her heels.

"You have to let go of everything," said Abigail.

Debbie Kay curled her arms around her legs until her knees buried her eyes. I could hear short clipped bursts of air escaping Little Eddie Onion's throat. I wondered if Mark Thomas was watching, hidden outside in the overgrown berry bush or buried beneath cobwebbed mountains of Runyon discards.

Fuller Street Agnes spoke to Abigail's back:

"Even God?"

Abigail turned a quick left and grasped Fuller Street Agnes by her plump, unblemished cheeks.

"Even God," said Abigail, and without so much as a warning, thrust her lips on her inquisitor's.

In bed, Abigail's picture in my left hand, my Baby Jesus night light turned off, the *West Side Story* album spinning in the background, I clutched at the crux of my pain until my stomach was sticky with achievement. When I finished, gasping, terrified my parents would spring open my bedroom door and admonish me with the torment of a mortal sin, I could not let go. I would not let go. I awoke soiled, still grasping Abigail's photograph.

I wish I could slow the story down here.

For the girls, kissing Abigail became a badge of honor, a calling card to a heightened awareness and an increased appetite for all things parentally forbidden. Liquor cabinets were raided, and booze was hoarded in cleaned-out margarine containers. Wild tales of wanton behavior, bared privates, and whispered intimacies circulated up and down our side streets. Chris Lee said the girls no longer went to confession, but we wondered how he knew, being Presbyterian. Girls began kissing girls on a semi-regular basis, first as shock technique, then, as Jenny described it later, "Because I needed to." Stephanie Regan was kicked out of her house when her mother discovered an all-girl slumber party had degenerated into what she referred to, amid peals of Italian, as a Roman orgy; Stephanie was forced to explore her new found hobby at her grandmother's. The Regan's basement had been the convergent spot for a flurry of Abigail's activities; the fact that it had a little bathroom off the laundry room hall made it perfect for kissing games that were increasingly circling the mythic bases. Mrs. Regan, a conservative Italian married to a square jaw of German descent, was the first and only parent to exercise any measure of control over Abigail's calculated chaos. Jimmy Festeri claimed to have kissed Stephanie's nipples on two occasions.

Mark Thomas laid low during the fall countdown, the stain of Woofer's untimely dismissal painted upon the swollen red crevices of his face. If the open homosexual activities of the fairer sex gained Markie any favors of his own with Little Eddie Onion or anyone else, Abigail and I knew little. Occasionally, we would spot a torn page from his sketch book: a monkey in heat, Father Hoskins, a girl with dirty blonde hair and a halo—all with their faces etched out with deeply grooved black slashes.

Abigail's relentless pursuit of my fears, combined with the very Catholic guilt of my nighttime exercises (I no longer even switched off the Baby Jesus night light), made the final weeks of summer vacation a jittery, spooky time. The Time of the Ghosts. If everyone in our neighborhood performed what was previously merely harbored, if Mark Thomas lurked behind every fireplug and holly tree, furiously scribbling away faces, I became a shadow—Abigail's shadow. Quiet and out of the way, I remained her constant companion—always a foot or so behind, which served a purpose, since the adults, in the advent of the egging and the explosive popularity of slumber parties, had become slightly edgier than usual, given the season. I tried to look out for my best friend.

The Time of the Ghosts was a time of opening locked doors and peering under beds way past midnight. Abigail knew my ghosts: heights and girls. I was terrified of being in high places, and I had never, besides my oh-so brief encounter with Abigail, kissed a girl. Not that I was ugly (and not that ugliness prevented Al Bossi from lying on top of Debbie Kay the better part of Seven Minutes in Heaven), but rather, my natural reticence, my shyness, my glory in regaling in my second-in-command post increased as every pore screamed for my lips to be next to my benefactor's.

"How about Alison?"

We were kicking along on an unnamed mission, a heavy brown supermarket bag sealed with electrician's tape thrust into my arms. Today was supposed to "Marys on the Lawn Day," but the Blessed Mother's name rarely came up these days.

"Alison? No way, José."

Abigail tore at a stick of gum.

"Half, stink-breath?"

"I'm rubber, you're glue. Whatever you say bounces off of me and sticks to you," I replied.

"Jenny?"

"She'd kill me first."

"I bet not. Crushes, crushes. Stephanie? She's cute."

"I thought she had a boyfriend now."

"Shame. She's a good kisser. But all that could change."

We had reached the edge of the woods and were doubling back along the fence line separating the fields from the backs of the houses. The air was cooler here, and the crunch of our footsteps set off a flock of birds behind us; otherwise it was silent. An unpleasant but not unfamiliar smell was creeping out of the bag.

"Fuller Street Agnes?"

"No no no. What's in the bag?"

"No to Fuller Street Agnes? She is kind of young, I guess, but it shouldn't matter. Nice boobs. Pretty teeth."

The bag smelled like farts, and I realized with a butterfly feeling that Abigail had not expelled gas in my direction for some weeks.

"The bag, Abigail. What's in the bag?"

"I think Joey Runyon kissed Alison again yesterday. Here, place the bag here."

I stopped short of a small hole filled with similar bags.

"Joey Runyon? What does she see in him?"

"How about a carved hockey player with a shot at first line center next year?"

"Alison likes that?"

"Ahh, Alison is it, my friend? Alison it is. Alison for you."

The hole had been hastily dug, and two plastic sand shovels were stuck in the tall crab grass. We were directly behind the Regan house. I could see Mr. Regan's buzzed hair atop his Frankenstein shaped head move up and down as he meticulously clipped his hedges.

"What are we doing with this stuff?"

Abigail pulled down her shorts and peed in the underbrush. A train was approaching in the distance, and another flock of birds flew startled into the crisp air.

"We nothing. You are putting your tongue in Alison's mouth, mister. Don't you worry about any of this. It's time to unleash, it's time to revel in it, it's time to start at the top to reach your bottom. Or Alison's."

I said nothing on the walk back home, but as I lay in bed, photograph in hand, images of Abigail peeing invading my every breath, I could visualize the strain in her eyes, the dark masses under her lids, the sheer force of will it took her to conceive a random act of violence—Woofer's execution via station wagon—in an otherwise extraordinary life. I did not touch myself that night. Instead, I made a resolution not to until Abigail returned to herself and an abiding sense of normalcy blanketed the raw desires of her mourning.

In the AM, there was church, but as we made our way out of the vestibule before communion to huddle beneath the stone stairs outside and smoke cigarettes (a Sunday ritual in our crowd), I took off and ran to the Avenue, weighed down by my Ziploc bag of coins and the money my mother gave me for the offering. There, at the Five and Dime, after much consideration (and much annoyance from ancient, bald Mr. Forty behind the counter), I selected a stuffed dog with a gas station patch that declared his name to be Henry. I cut across the Pike and walked along the Boulevard, careful to stay off the normal paths home from church.

Autumn was seeping into the breeze, and the slightest tinge of red heralded the change of seasons. I stowed Henry in the Runyons' garage and found the soon-to-be-Saint on the corner in a whispering circle of curly-haired girls. Abigail broke away from the crowd and grabbed my crotch.

"Where did you run off to?"

"Let me go. I'm not the only one who can keep secrets, you know."

She released my balls, and I fell to my knees.

"What did you do that for?" I gasped.

"Meet me tonight behind the Menkees' fence."

The circle of girls split into pairs and navigated their way past my dry heaving without passing a word. Abigail's red Sunday shoes were at eye-level, but I couldn't raise myself up to look at her face.

"Will you be there?"

"Okay, okay."

"Between the fences. After dark."

And the Sunday shoes were gone.

Harry Menkee was a modern man of means and, like Mr. Regan, took particular care of his lawn. He had erected a green mesh fence with shiny silver poles to surround his backyard, but his wife, his polar opposite (she was stick thin and conspicuously quiet, as if always listening for something in the distance; he was round and loud and smoked cigars), refused to allow him to remove the rusted posts and links from the original fence. Mrs. Menkee was an antique connoisseur—as if the sounds she were waiting for were clues to the history of the past. Therefore the back of Mr. Menkee's garage made a natural hiding spot—between the links with plywood mounted above.

There I waited, still in my church clothes, Henry still buried within the Runyons' garage. Slightly after nine, Abigail, in her soft purple dress and red Sunday shoes, climbed between the two fences and rubbed my face with onion grass. A small bruise the color of her dress decorated her neck.

"Sorry about before. I thought maybe you knew, and I didn't want you to mess anything up."

Abigail's face was older now, I thought. You could see where frown lines and laugh lines would someday adhere. Even her soft breath smelled exhausted and expired.

"Know about what? I had a surprise for you."

"I don't want you to get in any trouble. I don't want anything to take your mind away from Alison."

"Alison?"

"It's all been arranged."

Abigail squatted and leaned her back against the rusted fence. Normally, one would hear the sounds of freeze-tag or wire ball this time of night, the second-to-last weekend of the summer. But the children of this neighborhood, of Abigail's neighborhood, were into indoor games now. I hoped no one would find Henry in the Runyons' garage. As much as I wanted to pry what everyone knew except me from between her chapped lips, I knew I had to rescue Abigail tonight.

"It's my turn. Come on."

Abigail let me hold her hand, and we walked to the church and stood beneath the Hanging Tree. It was now the Time of Secrets, and my best friend in the whole world was swallowed within its slippery talons. I shucked my black dress shoes and tied the laces together.

"Here? You brought me here?"

"Take off your shoes," I said.

"My Sunday shoes?"

"Just take them off. They don't match your dress anyway."

Abigail lifted each foot, and I knelt in the street and removed her red shoes with care, tying the laces together.

"Okay Abigail, you have to make your wish."

"I don't need anything."

"Abigail, you have to make a wish."

"I don't want for anything."

"Yes you do. You want Woofer back. You need Woofer back or someone like him. Make your wish."

The top of Abigail's head, in her stocking feet, came to my nose; she was tall for a girl. She pushed her face into mine, and the bare remnants of bath oil drifted past. Without a glance, Abigail hurled her shoes into the air, and the laces struck the wire and held.

"Holy shit! If that means *anything*, your wish is about to come true."

I tossed my shoes, and the laces twirled around the wire on the first try.

"And your wish? What is your wish?" she asked.

Abigail's face was perilously close to mine again. Below the bath oil, I could smell the Doral cigarette she had outside the church, and I imagined her throat, the way it would constrict as if she were swallowing every last tendril of smoke. My hand strayed to the back of her neck, and I could feel my body heat up as if I was in a scalding shower.

Brushed, held, and…gently pushed away.

"You can't."

"I have to."

"I only kiss girls now."

My hand never left her neck.

"I'm in love with you."

"I can have you anytime. Don't you know I know that?"

"No you don't."

"I can make you do anything."

"No you can't."

"I only kiss girls now."

As if that were the final word, and with little effort, Abigail turned her head so my hand grasped nothing but night air. She was halfway down the block when she turned and mooned me.

"Tomorrow's your big day. Don't waste it all tonight."

But I did, despite my previous promise, rubbing it until it hurt, until my eyes burned from lack of sleep, Henry long forgotten in the Runyons' garage. And the next day, in Jenny's basement, the day before the Burning of the Poo, with my shorts pushed down, plump-around-the-middle Alison Hawkins shoved her fat little tongue down my throat, and I gagged and spit up into her mouth. Alison didn't seem to mind, her hands busy fondling my sore penis until Abigail, the future Saint Abigail of Rhawnhurst, stuck her head in the laundry room, took one look at my flaccid member, and yanked me, shorts still around my ankles, out through Jenny's garage.

"Well, so much for Alison Hawkins," Abigail said as if that solved anything.

Close to tears, I pulled my shorts up.

"Maybe you shouldn't play with it so much."

Our heads turned at a rustle in the bushes, and briefly a red map of a face blinked and disappeared. Mark Thomas. I was instantly convinced the whole crowd would know of my sexual faux pas.

"Listen, don't come out tomorrow night. Stay inside and read a book or listen to *West Side Story*. Don't come out, okay?"

I nodded and Abigail again took my hand, and we spent the rest of the afternoon in the cool air conditioning of the library, our heads almost touching, gazing at volume after volume of photography and art books. At night, we shared a bowl of popcorn and watched Johnny Carson, laughing even if we didn't get the punch lines, for we understood his impeccable timing—the timing was the thing. There is little doubt to me now that this was the proverbial calm before the storm.

Oh, to stop the narrative here—I know I'm in danger of falling behind—but for the record, Alison Hawkins doesn't count, only Abigail's kiss—it needs to be said.

The Burning of the Poo was an extremely well coordinated event involving, like my own personal egging incident, several fronts, including a few porches belonging to the alleged perpetrators. I was in my room, naturally, when the doorbell rang. I had spent most of the day alone, pouring over well-thumbed comic books and flipping sports cards for the umpteenth time. My neck was like a raw piece of ragged string, chewed-upon and rubbed against until only a shadow remained. I didn't know what Abigail had planned, and I was crushed to be so uninvolved in what was clearly a major operation. The sound of the doorbell shook me from my malaise, and I bounded down the stairs and beat my mother to the front door.

I could smell it before I turned the knob. I could hear cries of distress outside before I pulled the door away from the frame. My mother stared at the clock in the living room as if it held answers.

"Who's ringing this time of night?"

How was my mother to know we were out of time, that the whole fabric of the neighborhood was about to be torn asunder in shared grief and reunited over the holy figure of Saint Abigail, nascent lesbian and chief architect behind the Burning of the Poo?

Already one voice outside shrieked above the rest. Before I pulled open the front door, one voice already claimed this night as her own. My mother's keen ears caught Mrs. Regan's voice—not so much floating over the cool night air as becoming part of it, tearing a hole in the cloud cover and settling in as if to become a permanent resident.

"What in the Lord's name?"

The smell bounded into our living room as soon as I jerked the door. The supermarket bag was on fire, sparks igniting the worn welcome mat—similar fires flared on porches up and down our street, and judging from the clashing coming from behind our house, on Arthur Street as well. Mr. Menkee's bag was already extinguished, and he sat on his haunches, meticulously attempting to wipe the dog shit from his shoes. My mother was too swift to fall for the Burning of the Poo. During the minute in which I stared out at the flaming bags dotting each porch and front stoop as far as the eye could see, my mother filled a spaghetti pot with water and doused our own personal shopping bag of dog excrement.

I could hear it like a bell: Mrs. Regan's high keening, now underscored by blunt shouts for help. Mr. Menkee ran off his porch without his shoes, and his wife stood in the doorway, shouting to him that this was a fool's way to catch cold until her eyes settled on the sweatered lump of Mr. Regan spread-eagled beside still burning bags of poo.

Although it would have been easy to squeeze the younger children (and perhaps even most of the older ones, worn out now from three weeks of crossing the boundaries), Mrs. Regan and the other neighbors chose not to press charges or seek damages, despite rather strong objections from Mrs. Menkee. All in all, Abigail's secret ops managed to land flaming bags of dog turds on four blocks worth of porches and front steps. Most of the bags were easily extinguished; a few caused minor damage to doors or outdoor plants. One dog, Ernie, named after Hemingway, tried to push the bag off his porch using his nose, a brave effort to either save his owner's property or horde a bag of poop to sniff later at his convenience. His nose was severely singed, but Ernie, like our neighborhood, was ever stoic. We all learned to breathe through our mouths. Even the next day, the cool air carried the scent, and all the backyard dogs, originators of Abigail's ammo, howled in either indignation or triumph.

Whether Stephanie took part in planting poop on her own estranged parents' porch is debatable, but what is not is that their house was ground zero. The other four blocks worth of targets were red herrings. Only Mrs. Sara Bates' house was spared. The old woman stuck her head out and shouted something into that night's reek and din regarding Abigail's "lovely figure" and retreated. When Mr. Regan's heart constricted and then released him from his grounding, his physical fall to the porch was cushioned by a few of the forty-odd burning bags arranged around Mrs. Regan's two potted plants. Unlike Little Eddie Onion's similar descension into sewer waste, no one was around to save fastidious Mr. Regan. If Stephanie helped pass the bags in the poop brigade from the arms of one masked child to another (some wearing handkerchiefs over their mouths and noses, I was told), she never said a word, although Abigail's intended message to the only parents who dared interfere with the Time of the Dares was clear. It was Abigail's ultimate artistic statement. Stephanie moved back home the next day to care for her widowed mother, and I helped the kids, some of the same ones who planted the poop I supposed, toss the bags into the back of Mr. Runyon's pickup truck.

Abigail was instantly ostracized; no one knocked on her door to suggest a seemingly lazy afternoon game of Spin the Bottle, no one rang her phone to beg her to meet beneath the overhang behind the Russians' shed. There was no show of outward animosity, just the simple sound of connections broken when Abigail picked up the phone, just the most unbearable moment of being a kid suddenly on the outside. I spent many hours over the next few days circling her backyard, throwing pennies at her window from mine, masturbating furiously to her photograph. I thought that surely Abigail didn't lump me in with the rest of her disciples. But for three days, she remained buried in her room, surrounded by her books and her collection of Mary figurines. Abigail no longer read to the widow Sara Bates. I never saw the old lady again; she vanished from the story as Abigail neared her descension and swift ascension.

Flash forward: Someone touched her blanket, her worn piece of cloth distinguishable as a blanket only by the shiny satin ends, and walked again. While it is assumable that this penitent was lame at the start, no one I spoke to could positively identify who it was exactly. The wheelchair was on the front lawn, as was the custom, or so the story goes, and her mother had just gone inside not fifteen minutes after wiping the drool from her daughter's slack face, a ritual she performed hourly, when a loud shrieking commenced, and an old woman ran to the front door and screamed, "He can walk, he can walk, Blessed Mother, he can walk again." That's how it started: the whole thing began with a scream and ended with Little Eddie Onion's "only costs a dime" one-man tour of all things Abigail.

On the morning of the last Friday before the last weekend of our miserable summer, my mother's navy blue dress was laid out on her bed. She only wore the dress for funerals and weddings, and as I was unaware of any impending nuptials, the sheer force of Abigail's nighttime raid smacked my face and little droplets of sweat formed in the corners of my eyes. On top of all this, I was terrified of funerals; the mere thought of a dead body—in my mind, rapidly decomposing and laid out vampire style—chilled my hands to the point of no longer having fingers.

"Time to get dressed."

"I can't."

"Mr. Regan's wake was last night. The coffin will be closed."

"I can't."

"You will. Come on now, get dressed."

I dawdled as long as possible until I was forcibly escorted to my closet and handed my Sunday clothes. Of course, that's when it hit me. Shoes hanging. My good Sunday shoes were dangling from a wire on Hasbrook Avenue directly across from the church, mingling with various Abigail footwear. With great care, I eased out of my room, down the stairs (careful not to tread on the creaky fourth step), and ran to Abigail's house. I banged on the door with my knuckles and tried to compose myself if she answered. Instead, I faced her mother, already dressed for today's formal activities.

"Is Abigail home?"

Her mother eyed my untucked shirttails and shoeless feet, my socks already sooty from my hasty escape. She sighed deeply and allowed me to enter underneath her arm.

"Upstairs. She won't come out."

"Thank you."

"Maybe she'll talk to you. I had no idea she was this close to Stephanie's father."

"Yes, ma'am."

"And stop with the pennies. You're going to break the glass."

Abigail's bedroom door was locked. I spoke softly into the keyhole. I could hear *The Sound of Music* cast album spinning beneath the thumping in my chest.

"My shoes are hanging. My Sunday shoes."

There was no response but the needle lifted and Julie Andrews was silenced mid-phrase.

"Abigail, my shoes. I need them for the funeral. My mother, Abigail. She'll kill me."

Mark Thomas' bedroom door, positioned at a right angle from Abigail's, opened a crack, and I imagined I could smell sulfur emitting from behind his puss-filled face.

"I need my shoes."

Her brother slammed his door, and their mother yelled something from the first floor. I brought my lips to Abigail's keyhole.

Brushed, held, released.

"Get them yourself."

Abigail's voice was hoarse, as if she'd been crying.

"The Hanging Tree. I can't climb the tree."

Then nothing, then the sound of the needle on vinyl, then Abigail's belly suddenly at eye level.

"You don't have to kneel, mister. Today is your day. Today you conquer your last fear. I dare you. The Last Dare."

And with that, she burst into Markie's room (which smelled strongly of sweat socks), opened his window, and lowered herself from the overhang into the backyard.

"Excuse me," I said.

Mark Thomas lay on his bed in his underwear, charcoal drawings littered the room and various stained footwear stood at attention like chess pieces. I glanced briefly at the open window, stepped into the hall, and closed his door. Once again I spoke into a keyhole.

"Markie, don't tell, okay? I need my shoes."

Flash forward: And the people came: first in pairs or trios, then entire families, then entire neighborhoods it seemed. They lined the streets and snapped photographs and kneeled on the grass, beating their breasts, clutching rosary beads. Their voices rose and fell until after a few weeks, their noise became a piece of our street like cars passing by a bedroom window late at night or the sound of the train no one ever really heard anymore.

-Dear Lord, thank you for bringing the girl to us and thank you for your everlasting mercy and love, amen.

-You think the least they could do is put some coffee on.

-Come now. Aren't we a flock? Don't the laws of Moses forbid us to bow down and worship false gods?

-Can it, Father.

-Yeah, at least her parents aren't passing around a collection basket.

-Have you seen her shoes?

-Is this the line? Are we in line?

-No, but my sister's husband did. The red ones, right?

-Are we not all children of God? Can we not reason together as one?

-Can it, Father.

-Yeah, at least we don't have to confess to some gay old priest before we receive the light of the Lord.

The Hanging Tree was dead. Its branches reached toward the sky in some last middle finger to God. The roots burrowed under the spikes of the low church fence and reached almost to the asphalt walkway leading to the convent. There were no leaves, but I could almost imagine their skeletons piled somewhere, millions of the Hanging Tree's abandoned offspring, jettisoned to the ground, a mirror mockery to the stars.

I was crouched on the first branch, and Abigail was pushing with both hands on my butt. The wire looked a thousand miles away, my Sunday shoes gently swaying inches from the great beast of a tree. The plan was this: once I was close enough, Abigail would scale the branches below me and hand me a broomstick to free the shoes.

"You have to keep moving. Your mom's going to notice you're gone."

"I can't do this. The branches can't hold me."

"Just reach for the next one, close your eyes, and pull yourself up."

"I'm going to fall."

"I'm not going to let that happen."

"I'm going to die."

"I'll catch you. Now, keep moving. One branch at a time. You can do it."

I reached above my head, pieces of bark showering my hair, Abigail's firm hands now on my lower back, her voice like a distant radio in someone else's car.

"Just let go. Let everything fall beneath you as you rise up. Like muddy water in a clear glass. Let yourself rise above the muck."

"Thank you, Mrs. Bates."

I lifted my body and hunched, trembling, on the next limb. Hasbrook Avenue was already a distant dot to me. Abigail hanging upside down to retrieve the broomstick seemed to happen on another plane, her voice coming from a place deep within the killing floor. Below Abigail's mantras, I could hear a vehicle approaching in the distance and a blurred megaphone. When the produce man's junky truck whooshed down the street, the branches shuddered a response; I bit my lower lip and wet myself.

Flash forward: Little Eddie Onion, once the sparring partner of Abigail's brother, once the rescued recipient of her good fortune, took the entrepreneurial spirit ingrained by his savior and ran with it. His Abigail Tours cost only a dime and included a brief reenactment of the Sewer Incident (although Little Eddie Onion used old tennis balls, his fears of the sewer unabated—his business acumen notwithstanding), a quick tramp through my backyard to her hiding place between the Menkees' fences, and finished with a flourish beneath the Hanging Tree, her red shoes and sneakers twisting in the autumn air. Despite the relative brevity of the tour (and the sightseers occasionally having to fend off an angry Mr. Menkee), business boomed for Little Eddie Onion. Word on the street was that the girls, led by Fuller Street Agnes and Debbie Kay, were busying themselves by fashioning soon-to-be-released holy cards.

I peed in Abigail's hair. It leaked out from beneath my good trousers and dripped to the limbs below. Between tears, sweat, and pee, I was sure I would die from dehydration before I fell to my death on Hasbrook Avenue. Abigail merely wiped her face on her sleeve.

"Abigail, please. I can't do it. I'm scared."

"Maybe today's not your day after all."

"Can you please let me down?"

"You can come down whenever you want, mister. I would never do anything to hurt you, don't you know that?"

"Can you please get my shoes for me?"

Pause. In retrospect, the longest pause I have ever known.

"Sure. Just put your weight on my shoulders and let yourself down."

Once I was secure on Hasbrook Avenue, Abigail wedged the broom handle between two branches above her and scaled the Hanging Tree, hands over feet.

"You just have to let go, mister man. You have to let go of *everything* and then you can climb *anything*."

Flash forward: The photograph is still on my nightstand, but I no longer masturbate to her smiling face. My mother asked me one morning (after I awoke crying) if I thought maybe I should put the picture away for a while, but I shook her off. The crinkled edges and the little bends in one corner make the image seem like it was stolen from some lost tribe a hundred years ago.

And today, at daybreak, I made my decision—I've written it all down first as you can see—today I decided to let go.

Back: Abigail hung upside down and grasped the broom handle between her fingers. I hadn't seen her so vivid in weeks; her smile swallowed her face, and it was all I could to do to keep from laughing as she swooped from limb to limb singing "These Are a Few of My Favorite Things." When she reached the branch closest to the wire, all I could see were the soles of her Chucks.

"The trick here, mister, is not to get electrocuted."

"Electricity can travel through wood?"

"Well, since your unfortunate bladder release, things are slightly damp where I'm concerned."

Abigail's arms swung the broom handle like a stickball bat and connected with the shoes. The wire shook violently for a moment.

"Maybe you should try and hook them with it," I yelled to her Chucks.

"Maybe you should try draining the vein before taking your life in your hands."

And I laughed in spite of the danger of getting caught in the Hanging Tree, in spite of having soiled my Sunday trousers. My best friend was back and in charge. All the pain since the Burning of the Poo was released into the coming autumn air each time Abigail cracked wise.

"*When the dog bites, when the bee stings, when I'm feeling sad—*' Look out!"

The broomstick went smacking down the tree and somersaulted into the street. I ran and retrieved it, Mr. Regan's funeral now seemingly a part of someone else's story.

"Shit shit shit."

Still laughing, I said, "I thought we had to let go of everything."

Abigail doing Mae West: "Not everything, big boy. Toss it up my way."

Flash to now: She is in a permanent state of sleep not unlike Dorothy in the field of poppies. Only, fat chance our hero will ever awake. She cannot move and drools like an infant. Her arms are stark white slabs of useless meat, and her cheeks sag under the weight of her torpor. I creep into the backyard and inch my way alongside her parents' garage. Typically, when the autumn sun beats down at its strongest, she is wheeled in under the cool dampness of the garage while the faithful mill impatiently in the street.

And there she is: a reeking lump of flesh fastened into a wheelchair by two belts. I place Henry the dog in her lap and brush the hair out of her eyes. All of this seems to take place outside of myself, and a great yawning of nothingness seeps up from my toes and exits through the tears plowing my face.

"I love you."

And I kiss her sweaty forehead.

Brushed, held, released.

And her eyes open to follow mine, and I stare back until her lids slowly close.

Back back back to then:

The broomstick was in her hand again, and the tip just about reached the laces of my Sunday shoes.

Us together: "*...I simply remember my favorite things, and then I don't feel sooo bad!*"

Abigail: "I don't think—"

The branch Abigail was standing on cracked, and there she was: her hands stretched above her grasping the next limb, her body hovering over the church fence. The broomstick shuttled to the ground. The broken branch followed behind.

"Holy shit. Abigail!"

"It's nothing, hoss."

"Don't let go. Help! Oh my God, Abigail. Whatever you do, don't let go. Do not let go!"

"I'm okay, I'm okay. I'll just swing myself over, and it'll be done. Don't wet your pants. Oops, too late."

When the limb she was dangling from snapped, Abigail laughed, and her body bounced off the church fence and flopped into the churchyard, her spine and legs posed like an unnatural question mark. In the distance, the produce man shouted something about strawberries, and a block over, my mother was stepping into a navy blue dress, and somewhere, deep inside my chest, something died.

It is now:

I can't reach the second branch, and there is Mark Thomas, his eyes drilling me over, his hands stained with charcoal, his face about to burst from the pressure of all his pimples. I am frightened to be caught so naked, so unprepared, climbing the Hanging Tree in my bare feet to get a better grip, Hasbrook Avenue already so far away, although I'm only on the first branch. I have a steak knife, but I don't know if I can use it on Abigail's brother.

Mark Thomas swiftly grasps the limb I am hunched on and pulls himself above me.

"Here."

Markie's strong, worn hands lattice together, and I place my foot into his callused palms. We climb this way until the branches get smaller, and I continue as I have to, as Mark Thomas knows I have to: alone.

"Here."

I look down and Markie pulls a piece of paper from his pocket and unfolds it so I can see. It is Abigail, smiling, holding Woofer, her eyes signaling to someone to her left, her gaze seeing no boundaries between being a sketch and being real. It's a picture perfect ending, I think. Abigail would have liked that line. She would have liked this one too: I am letting go.

"It's for you."

Mark Thomas drops to the ground and leaves the sketch under the Hanging Tree. Barefoot, I edge across the branch just below the wire, holding anything above my head for balance, ignoring the two splintered branches—Abigail's branches. The steak knife is wet against my palm.

I exhale and reach,

      exhale and reach,

           exhale and reach,

                exhale and cut down the red shoes hanging.

-end-

Lord's Finger

"A storm is threatening my very life away
If I don't get some shelter, oh yeah, I'm gonna fade away."
The Rolling Stones, "Gimme Shelter"

Recommended Soundtrack:

"So What" by Miles Davis

"Gimme Shelter" by the Rolling Stones

"Loverman" by Metallica

I indulge myself in every desire known to man. I smoke cigarettes until my throat pleads for relief and my tongue is like the tattered mat in front of my house. I drink liquors and wine until I vomit. Drugs—yes!—I swallow and snort and inject whenever I please and allow the chemical magic to seize all five of my senses. And women: all shapes and sizes and colors, two at a time, three at a time, in the most unnatural ways my polluted soul can conjure. Money is not a problem, and with the right amount, indulgences are plentiful and easily attained. The curtains are drawn, and I am sitting in my own shit. There is but one desire I will not satisfy: I will not write. I will not put pen to paper. And in this, as in all things, I defy Him.

Now how is this the truth, you say? Is not before you a collection of words and punctuation and ideas? I allow myself this one digression; I grant myself one reprieve from abstinence, for this is a tale that in its telling illuminates my war on Him. It is imperative the story sees the light of someone's eyes, if only to explain what remains of my own slowly dimming flame. Not that I seek an end to misery. On the contrary, I intend to inhabit this particular stasis if only to spit in the eye of God. Or break His hand.

+

I was a God-fearing man; it was the way I was raised. My parents were lower-middle-class merchants struggling up the cruel ladder of success when I made my appearance some years after they had surrendered the thought of ever bearing a child. During my early school years, my parents would tuck me into bed and tell me of my birth, of how they would spend hours staring at the little wriggling fingers so perfect in detail, miniatures of an adult's hands. The hands of God, they would say; "God's little miracle," they would call me.

It seems natural to me now that I would be a writer. An only child, frequently alone after school while my parents sought a better, more financially stable life for me, crayons led to paints, and they in turn to the oak desk complete with a little side typing table. There my mother would work out the family bills and my father could frequently be heard conducting business from its black telephone. Never actually forbidden from the desk, I knew it belonged to the grown-up world and therefore seemed out of reach. It was its shiny cluster of pens festooned in a holder like so many feathers on a peacock that led me to the life of a writer. I could not resist the pull of the pens. One grand afternoon, with a full two hours alone stretched before me like an ocean, I climbed the creaky chair, unearthed a glorious blank piece of typing paper, and emancipated both a variety of pens and my own tumescent imagination. Already well versed by the third grade, having been read a selection from a children's classics series each bedtime for years uncountable, my first effort was a veiled rewrite of Mark Twain's celebrated frog. My hero was a bluebird.

When my parents' car rolled into the driveway, I hid my story, having once been chastised by the nuns in school for creating an amusing comic strip that was distributed to my classmates and traded like contraband. My mother was crushed when the sister called and asked her to pick me up; I feared similar disappointment if the tale of the bluebird were to be discovered. My hands gave me away this time; they were covered in inks: brilliant blues, explosive reds, determined blacks. My mother asked me how I passed the afternoon hours, and I lied until she knelt before me and held my hands. Trembling, I unearthed the little story. A few tense minutes passed, my father reading over my mother's shoulder, their eyes cruising the multicolored second-hand adventures of a rather notorious bluebird. Instead of the punishment I expected, my parents were ecstatic— they cried. My father lifted me off the ground, and my mother held my hands in front of her face. I can still smell her light perfume.

"The hands of God," they said, "the little hands of God."

My parents encouraged and invited me into a world of words long before my classmates ever heard of Shakespeare or Melville or Hardy. I would climb a tree in the backyard and read until my mother called for supper. They assisted me in my initial submissions to literary magazines. I knelt in church and before my bed praying to God, asking for greatness if He so desired. I invoked His name with every syllable. Though my parents bought me a typewriter, all first drafts were composed solely with strokes from a pen. I wanted to be closer to the words; I desired to feel His breath upon my neck. My parents sent me to a private high school and paid for the best college. Without such love, I believed, my life would surely have been on a different and wholly unsatisfying path.

+

I wish I could say my initial success was due to a long and difficult struggle. The opposite is true. The arduous task of waking at five each morning to face the blank page was more strenuous than placing pen to paper. I considered myself a conduit for God. Out of college, the rejection slips ceased altogether, and my first novel, a long-winded but sincere account of my initial adventures with the opposite sex, was picked up by a fairly reputable publishing house and sold respectably. The second book, a seriocomic treatise on mental illness based on a college roommate's frequent sabbaticals in our state's finer psychiatric facilities, was a bestseller.

My parents died young, victims of an automobile accident—while on their way to pick up their whiskey-soaked only child from a post-college gathering of literary types, their car hit a patch of black ice and skidded into a thicket of trees. I tried to write my sorrow away. I was a bachelor, married to the word, which I found more comforting than any flesh and blood companion. Flush with money from the sale of my novels and living in the house of my youth, I suppose the sheer size of my loss and my inability to tackle the tragedy of God's violent call to my parents led me to what is often referred to as the number one occupational hazard of writers: alcoholism.

The drink was sneaky. It started on days when I found myself small again in my father's chair, facing the old wooden desk with its little side typing table. The drink bolstered my sense of place in the world but derailed the narrative of my third book, the veiled story of my parents' journey from destitute immigrants to saviors of a kind, insistent upon raising me with every available amenity, allowing the flower to bloom in a hothouse of artistic appreciation. It was their faith that caused me to doubt. Could the God of my parents be a loving and merciful God and yet not allow them to glow under the virtuous fruition of their only son? I drank like the heroes of the word my father worshipped in his youth—the lost generation that emerged in the 1920s. I allowed wine and gin to taint the blood of my father and wash away my inherited worship of God.

It didn't take long, of course, to run through the money, and before I fully grasped the gravity of the situation, my work took a distant second to a severe dedication to the bottle. I stopped going to church; I ceased all prayer. Lying in bed, I waited for wanton dreams—for the liquor inhibited the physical act of love. And it was in a dream that the hand of God directed me once more and led me eighty-three miles from my home in Mondauk Proper to the land of promise and honey disguised as a little seaside town called Lola-by-the-Sea.

The dream was cinematic and spooled off in a slightly tinted, noirish black and white. Three shopworn scribblers, a grizzled Ernest, a frail Francis, a stubborn William—barflies all—vied for dominance, mired in the throes of their addiction. I stood witness to their devotion to something other than the craft. William sat at the end of the bar, his chin hovering above an empty glass, peering out of the corners of his eyes toward the rowdy table in the crook of the room. Ernest was holding forth there, Francis and three women and another man hanging on his every word. Francis' face was drawn, and his skin was pale; he appeared to require a huge effort not to fall off the chair.

William spoke to me first as I entered stage left—a bartender with ink on his hands.

"Can you ask them to keep it down?" he drawled. "There's a writer in the room attempting to recover."

He banged his empty glass on the bar, overturning a full ashtray, and I could see the worn spots on his sport jacket, could smell the years of liquor on his breath. Then the barmaid was there: long dark hair, a nose that slanted to a point, eyes full of tales not told. William paid no attention to her as she swept the ashes and leaned over the bar to touch my arm.

"You're new, but you'll get used to it. I'm Hezza. We've been waiting for you. When it's over, you'll have to wash yourself in the ocean, but I'll have a dry towel and hot tea for you. It'll be okay."

Hezza served round after round to Ernest's table, and for the first time I noticed the smell of salt in the air. I strained to hear the waves surrender to the beach. The patrons filtered out until only Ernest and a swaying Francis remained seated—William still held an unsteady guard barside. Ernest continually placed his palm over the flame of the candle centered on the table. Francis maintained a steady laugh that sounded like bones rolling down a hill, keeping his eyes on Hezza as she cleared empty glasses.

"Should I start cleaning up?" I asked Hezza, her hands now buried in the sink.

"No, we're not finished yet," Ernest's voice boomed. "Where is he? Tell him it's time!"

William descended from his bar stool and approached Ernest's table. "Arm wrestling first?" William asked, and Francis puked in his own lap.

"It starts with this," Hezza said as she gazed over the writers with a not-altogether-disapproving look. "Indian wrestling will be next, and then a bit of boxing, even though Ernest has almost five inches and fifty pounds on him."

Francis used his tie to clean the vomit off his shoes. "Don't worry about Francis. He'll drink himself sober in a few hours and leave to meet his wife. She needs him. But he can't resist the temptation to be here with Ernest," Hezza explained. I nodded.

"Why are you here?" I asked.

"For the words," she replied.

Ernest struck William off balance. Francis sipped a drink, and in a deeply slurred voice, informed me that no one ever calls him by his first name in the real world. "I'm c-c-called Scott."

"It is good to know one's true name," Ernest said after he took a pull from a bottle of rum.

"Nicknames are vulgar," William said as he picked himself off the floor and eyed the rum. "It's what you're made of that—"

"Flesh and blood," Ernest said, pounding his chest.

"Or paint and canvas," William retorted. "As long as you know, who cares what your *true* name is?"

"*Still* c-c-called Scott," Francis managed before collapsing on the table. Ernest and William began circling each other warily, as they passed a bottle back and forth.

Hezza stroked my arm again. "It's time to clean you off. The last competition involves a measuring of sorts that no one needs to see— not sober at least. Sometimes they want to see who's bigger; other times it's about who can maintain it longer."

Her laugh was like cold clear water cascading past moss-covered rocks, and when she kissed me, I could taste saltwater on her tongue.

"Where am I?"

"Lola-by-the-Sea."

I disrobed behind the building, and the ocean stretched in front of me, barely visible in the darkness. "I'll be over there," Hezza said, gesturing toward a jumble of shadows. The water was warm and my bones felt at ease. I swam for what felt like hours, until I could no longer see the shore, just the outline of Hezza standing on a rock jetty. I swam toward her, and I could hear her voice over the waves in my ears. I yelled in return and pushed my body further. My arms were useless and numb, flaying at the foam. Hezza's voice above the water as my feet touched the first slippery rocks: "Say my name."

I climbed the side of the jetty, whose end curved slightly like half a shepherd's crook, and Hezza was waiting for me naked. Hezza said, "Say my name," and I did. I reached for her and she was gone. A wet towel and a cold mug of tea were on the rock, and I awoke shivering, my blankets soaked in night sweats, my head buzzing, my voice hoarse from shouting her name.

+

I sold my parents' house and all of their belongings. I took only the oak desk. After renting a small truck, I traveled the northeastern coastline in search of a house on the beach near a rock jetty that ended in an aborted curve. Negotiations for the paperback rights to my novels were completed. The dream was God's wake-up call, and I answered with vigor.

Lola-by-the-Sea was not listed on any map, but the name sounded familiar, and after ingratiating myself with various locals (and finding myself at the losing end of several "just down the road a mile or two" directions), I reached a spit of a town hidden between more prominent beachheads. It took all of an hour to find my home—when I walked up the stony path leading to the obviously long-abandoned white dwelling, my stomach danced. The house was roomy and worn by the sea air and storms; its wooden floors moaned a story with each footstep, and its little balcony overlooked a narrow beach. A half-mile to the north, a rock jetty jutted into the ocean; waves lapped at the slight curve at its end in a vain attempt to repel it back to land. It was there I headed after inspecting the house.

On the far side of the beach I came upon some fishermen cleaning their reels and cages. I introduced myself and, after some banter and the passing around of a bottle, I pried into their town's history, eager for tasty tidbits before meeting again with the realtor. I wanted to assure myself that this blot, this sparse gathering of forgotten souls nestled against the waves, was in fact my destined endgame.

The fishermen winked and nodded and regaled me with the story of Lola, a pretty young thing, they said, with fiery hair and a strawberry birthmark on her left cheek. Led by an old hand whose white hair set off a face sunk below hard wrinkles, the fishermen spun the tale, each speaking in turn, and the sun receded from the overcast sky.

"Lola married young to a promising but infantile fishing lord whose father just about owned this town," began the man with the white hair, his voice cracking like the spine of an old book.

"Infantile? Showing off your education there, Jack Woods?" asked someone, and everyone laughed as if this was a familiar jibe.

"She'd been born into the poor stock that made their living fishing for her future husband's family," the first man continued, without losing a beat. "Lola worked as a caroler, singing in the various pubs that used to cling to this beach line, entertaining laborer and landowner alike." Jack paused to inspect his pipe.

"At least that's what they called her—Lola—but some said that weren't her Christian name."

The man's parents did not approve of Lola and her background, the fisherman explained, but could not deny her stunning beauty or the way their eyes could not leave the strawberry birthmark. Nor could they ignore her extraordinary singing voice. The men gathered before me all agreed her song could call the fish to surface. But there came a time, during their first year of marriage, when the husband happened upon Lola among some of his employees, "enjoying a story and a laugh much in the way we are, lad," someone explained, his face hidden behind a crab trap.

"The husband was checking on his father's boats and was embarrassed by Lola's cavorting—he was in the company of several other young businessmen, you understand," explained one of the fishermen, his hands busy coiling an extremely worn rope.

"He created quite a stir in the sand and fired several of the laborers until one of his friends laid a hand on his shoulder and asked if he wasn't overreacting to a small situation," Jack said between honks into a gray handkerchief, his pipe still bobbing in the corner of his wrinkled mouth. "The young man relaxed, but then one of his companions sealed Lola's fate with a few words: 'Besides, a great beauty like Lola's needs sunshine and good friends. How else could ill mannered men like ourselves drink in her good looks if you always have her locked in that oversized house of yours?' The other businessmen laughed but Lola's companions recoiled. Without a word, the son of the fishing magnate slapped Lola in the mouth and dragged her from her friends, locking her in their great white house on the beach." Jack relit his pipe.

"Magnate, Jack?" asked a man wearing a faded green hat pulled over his eyes.

"There she remained for the next few years," Jack said; only the maid could verify ever seeing her: "just a flash of red hair and a mumbled thank you as the meal tray was shoved into the hall."

Jack's white hair stood bold against the red bowing of the sun.

"The beach front was full of rumors regarding the current fate of Lola," he continued. "It enveloped the whole town. Her parents moved away in the middle of the night.

"It wasn't until October of the third year of her imprisonment, during what our fathers' fathers called Deep Autumn—just after the clocks are turned back and darkness seems to eat away the sun—that the tale of Lola reached its denouement."

Jack cleared his throat: "All through the night, the laborers heard screaming and the sound of glass shattering from the white house. A few fishermen gathered on the beach amid the reeds with a bottle between them. Just past two in the morning, a naked Lola burst through the back door and scurried down the beach.

"The men who saw her, lad, well, they never forgot it, did they?" said the man cleaning the crab trap. "The left side of her face was covered in bandages; where her strawberry birthmark would have been, there was just gauze and tape. Lola sprinted to the jetty, the husband in his shirtsleeves close behind. Without regard to the broken shell splinters and pointy rocks, Lola ran the length of the jetty and plunged into the water.

"And that was the end of that, one would think," the man finished, a pained look on his face, "but they never found her body."

Jack coughed and squinted into the dying sun: "The husband grew into madness, and each night, even through a rough winter, he stood upon the jetty screaming her name. The family eventually had him institutionalized and closed shop on our little town."

How it had come to officially be named Lola-by-the-Sea, no one knew, but in October, during Deep Autumn, the fishermen swore Lola's song could be heard just below the sound of the ocean, and her white outline could be seen on the crook of the jetty.

Each of the men watched my face for reaction when the tale concluded.

"Sounds like a bit of Hawthorne wrapped up in there," I said, and Jack tapped the bowl of his pipe with his calloused fingers.

"That house there, the one you're looking at? Well, that was his. Ought to know about it before you buy it," he said. "One of the fishermen who saw her that cold, cold night was a cousin of mine."

"And those rocks there," I asked, pointing, "that jetty, I suppose that's where Lola came to her unfortunate end?"

Jack puffed on his pipe and held my gaze for longer than I liked. "Ayup. That's the Lord's Finger, and this is Lola-by-the-Sea. Ought to know."

I jumped up and pointed again. "That is the Lord's Finger?" I asked.

"Ayup," was the reply, and I bought the house the next day. God had pointed the way in my dream and now gave me a sign; I had reached the promised land, and I was free.

+

Safe from myself, my fiction turned a corner. I abandoned the novel I had attempted to construct while in my cups and focused on the short form. Every morning and every night before I put pen to paper, I would walk to the point of Lord's Finger and give thanks to Him for my gift; I would praise His name into the ocean spray and return to my father's desk refreshed and inspired. Even the focus of my new stories evolved from thinly disguised accounts of my own life to man's search for perfection, the sufferer's search for the Almighty. I believed the hand of God touched me. He wrote through me, not in the Gospel sense, but in the way He stroked the pen and allowed my gift to flourish. My characters strived to see His face and achieved the impossible only when they realized He was beneath every rock and high atop every tree, burrowed within the roots and one with the rain. I did not need to drink; my love of Him was intoxicant enough.

I understood the tragedy of my parents' accident and no longer blamed Him. If all occurrences are part of His plan, then their death led me to Lola-by-the-Sea and my redemption. I was without doubt. My only trial was loneliness, and in the throes of my bodily struggle, I sang His name. There is nothing without sacrifice, and seclusion was mine. My fiction was sold to the best magazines, and my novels were selling again. I was spreading His faith in an innocuous way. I didn't need a pulpit or a church; I only needed a pen. I could satisfy my urges alone, fortified with the knowledge that my work would be remembered. I hung a postcard of a youthful Jack Kerouac on the wall next to my bed, his arms spread before a rapt audience, his head titled in such a way as to suggest both humility and utter arrogance. Whenever the call of the flesh overwhelmed me, I would look at the postcard: here was a man who had the gift and buried it beneath layers of drugs and alcohol and sex, here was a man without God. I lived solely to immerse myself in the craft.

+

At night I dreamed of Hezza; I dreamed of her touching my arm and kissing my mouth. She was both my angel and tormentor. In my dreams, Hezza was marked with a spot of strawberry on her left cheek, and she danced with me on the rocks of Lord's Finger. I would awake with her name on my lips.

On those rare nights when I couldn't intellectualize my desires away or dull them with my faith, I would explore the house. After some research in the library located in the next town over, I discovered the young prince of fishmongers had in fact resided in my house. He had been a painter before his father had pressed him into service, and there were two mentions of college showings. However, there was no mention of Lola or marriage in any of the newspapers I dredged up on microfiche. All through the house, every closet except the one in the master bedroom and the one located at the foot of the stairs near the front door was sealed with padlocks. The realtor was not familiar with any of the former inhabitants (and was maybe too lazy to call a locksmith or perhaps he thought sealed closets gave the house even more mystique), so on those nights when sleep escaped me, I hammered the locks off and briefly entered into other people's lives. The closets were mostly filled with books and old galoshes, but rummaging through them gave me a satisfaction I could not quite explain and at the same time left me feeling disappointed. With every hammer blow, I expected to come face to face with the art of the fish magnate's son. Each room had at least two closets, so the anticipation grew with each opening, but still I discovered nothing.

Hezza found her way into my fiction, the earthly savior of the struggling protagonist. Every girl in every story was Hezza—this angel of the truth, an aid in the heroes' search for the sacred. Whenever she appeared, it was like greeting an old friend. No stranger to temptation and unashamed of it, Hezza touched the hero's arm and reminded him of the perfection in the imperfections of a leaf, reminded him of the task ahead if only he allowed the water to rise above the mud. In my own way, I loved Hezza, and as much as I longed for someone like her in my life, I hid this wish from God and buried her in words.

+

I frequently took meals at a pub some blocks from my house called the Maidenhead. I always sat in the last wooden booth, near a bandstand that never seemed to be in use, making notes in a black journal, honing the many ideas down to a few. The clientele were local residents mostly, and my presence neither disturbed nor interested them. It was there I met Hannah Lee.

Hannah Lee was tending bar and keeping conversation flowing, filling this patron's glass, flirting with a man wearing a hat covered in lures. Her long hair was dark and tied back by a red ribbon, her clothes—fashionable but inexpensive—carelessly worn over her slim body. Her complexion was fair. There were no signs of any birthmarks.

I had eaten at the Maidenhead two or more times a week for almost two years, and our paths had never crossed, but she was clearly not a recent hire; her familiarity with the customers gave her away: the way she touched this one's hand or looked cross when another, obviously intoxicated, requested a last round. She seemed to float on air behind the bar, effortlessly moving from task to task. When she took her break, Hannah Lee switched sides, perched on a bar stool, and read a rumpled paperback. She sipped from a sculpted green mug that appeared handcrafted. The economy of motion used to transform from diligent barkeeper to studious reader made my hands tremble. I almost left without paying my tab.

I could think of nothing else in bed but her face, the laugh wrinkles around her eyes, the slightly upturned nose, the way she bit her lip while she read, her fingers playing piano along her chin. I did not write a word the next day. I walked the length of the house, up and down the stairs. I played Miles Davis' *A Kind of Blue* repeatedly until I thought the needle would dig grooves into the vinyl. I stood on Lord's Finger and said aloud the name I heard the taproom men use: Lee.

The following day, I ironed my clothes twice and played solitaire for hours until the time to leave. After carefully counting backwards, I reasoned only two days of the week besides Sunday that I did not frequent the bar. I only hoped she would be working.

The Maidenhead was its usually sparse self with a few dinner customers but nary a bar stool empty.

"Hi, hon," said a waitress who recognized my face. "Didn't expect to see you tonight. Regular table is empty. I'll get a menu."

I wanted to ask after Lee, but if she was in the back and came out to see who I was, I had nothing to say. The meal was miserable and the journal remained closed. At half past eight, a draft from the back door blew on my neck, and Lee entered carrying her mug. A mounted coat rack was behind me in an alcove with a cigarette machine, and Lee breathlessly hung her jacket and tied her hair back.

"You're late again, Lee."

"I couldn't put the book down. I'm sorry, Lou."

And there she was, less than an arm's length from me, tying a black apron around her blue jeans.

"Did you make the mug?"

Hannah Lee turned, and I held my gaze; the temperature in my body rose alarmingly.

"The mug. Did you make it?"

"Yeah. It was for a class. I wish it wasn't so green, but I guess if I really wanted to change the color, I would have painted it by now." She laughed and went to work behind the bar.

Large sweat stains appeared under my arms, and I felt feverish. I could do nothing but write in my journal until my fingers cramped. I revised the poem ten times, and when I walked to the bar, I was surprised to see the stools nearly empty.

Hannah Lee's hands were submerged in a little sink. Her mug and book, Kierkegaard's *Fear and Trembling*, were at the end of the bar. I cleared my throat and handed her the poem.

"Are these words for me?" Hannah Lee asked, startled, dish water dripping from her arms.

"Yes. I just wrote them tonight."

"Well, then. If they're mine, can I read them now?"

"Here? Well. You can do whatever you please with them. It's about your green sculpture."

"My green tea mug?"

"Yes. I didn't know anything else about you."

The barmaid unfolded herself into a stool, and her eyes devoured my little work, sucking every bit of soul from each syllable.

When finished, she said, "My name is Hannah Lee. Everyone calls me Lee."

"Did you like the poem?"

"You're walking me home, aren't you?"

+

God had given me my Hezza. I could ask for nothing more. Lee moved into the white house by the sea two weeks after I had given her the poem. With Lee came hundreds of books, and we built sturdy wooden shelves along the wall of one room to house them. She arrived with little else, and during our nightly shell hunts along the shore, I learned that she stumbled into Lola-by-the-Sea with even less. Escaping a degrading marriage to a struggling stocks-and-bonds man who expected her to clip his toenails and dominated her every move, and without any living family to turn to for aid, Hannah Lee traveled southeast from her adopted hometown of Philadelphia, itself northeast of her birthplace in New Orleans, and settled in the little sea town when her car died, undignified and smoking, along a little used access road bordered on either side by overgrown vegetation with a rancid seashore smell. She was a painter and a sculptor with little ambition—meaning that Lee didn't care if anyone ever viewed the finished product; she existed merely to create. Lola-by-the-Sea seemed to her as good a place as any to find a job and fashion her pottery, paint her pictures.

We transformed the little room with the books into a studio. My writing room was across the hall, and we dragged the stereo upstairs to the walkway between, although to be honest, I did little writing. I structured my life around Hannah Lee and fretted away the hours she tended bar by staring at her paintings, running my fingers over her sculptures. Her series of watercolors depicting the temptation in the Garden of Eden were startling, and I mused for hours over the kind of mind that could capture the malevolence of the snake in a few fluid brush strokes.

I told Lee everything about me and my parents and my struggles—with the exception of Hezza. God flowed through my pen, and my pen transformed Hezza from a dream angel into breathing fiction. I didn't tell her that God brought her to me. I didn't tell Hannah Lee I thought I might have created her.

One cold February morning, a few months after Lee moved in, she kicked me awake and nearly shoved me off the bed with her feet. Her voice was slurred from sleep, and her eyes were closed.

"Time to write, dearheart. The desk is down the hall. I believe you know the way."

And so I wrote again, this time with a depth I had never imagined before. Every morning Lee kicked me out of bed, and I wrote six stories in six weeks. After dinner, Lee would suck in my words, biting her lip, her fingers playing piano along her chin. At times she would read them aloud, and her voice, a curious mixture of dialects as if she belonged to no one place, turned every paragraph into a polemic, and we would discuss the fine details until we fell into bed. That is how I remember those weeks: a continual falling in and out of bed.

+

Hannah Lee had heard the stories of Lola and the fisherman prince but not in such detail. She became fascinated with Lola, even briefly flirting with dying her hair red, an idea I was quick to squash. My own obsession with the story had waned. There were still a few closets locked, and I had yet to do more than poke my head into the attic. Lee desired more, and I dutifully showed her the few artifacts the library held. She pestered me to open the remaining closets, and after some protest, I hammered the locks away. The contents held no hint of Lola.

One morning Lee climbed into the attic. Her footsteps echoed through the house, and there followed the sound of something heavy falling from a long height. I stopped writing and ran to the attic ladder. Lee's head poked from the opening.

"Are you okay? I thought something happened to you." I was breathless.

"No, just trying to grab your attention, dearheart. Give me a hand, will you? And bring some candles."

The attic was a cobwebby, moist affair. Moldy boxes were piled high on wooden chests, and a large plywood crate leaned against the far wall where the roof was at its height. Poor ventilation made it difficult to breathe, and my neck ached from being hunched over. Lee opened box after box and analyzed the contents.

"More books. This town had its own library and didn't even know it. Look at these shoes."

I attempted to pry open the crate, but there must have been hundreds of nails all along its border.

"Easter hats. Oh and a fedora. Old magazines. Nice candlesticks."

"I'm starting to feel queasy from the smell, Lee. Can we finish tomorrow?"

"We could stay here for a week and never finish. A statue of a monk. Make that two monks."

"Lee, let's get something to eat."

"Look, it's one of those wind-up monkeys with the little cymbals. Jesus Christ."

Lee had wedged opened a rusty sea trunk. Inside were stacks of paintings on stretched canvases, each signed by Leslie Van Ark.

"Oh my God, that's him! These are his paintings. Bring the candles closer."

I held the light, and Lee lifted canvas after canvas from the trunk. There were studies of apples and oceans, and a series of sunsets.

"I can see why his parents wanted him to look after the fish. He wasn't very good was he?"

Lee held a small framed canvas in front of her face. She didn't say anything for almost a minute.

"No, but this one has something. Look, here on the back, he penciled the title. 'The Promise' "

In the painting, two hands were clasped together, one tan, adorned with an overly large ring, the other light complexioned.

"It's Lola's hand. I bet it's from when they first met."

I promised Lee we would finish tomorrow, and after we resealed the attic, Lee hung the painting of the hands in our bedroom directly across from our bed. I didn't object.

+

The morning after the attic adventure, Lee kicked me out of bed, and I slumped into the writing room and slept on the couch. I rarely used the typewriter except for final drafts, so I knew she wouldn't question what I was doing. When I heard Lee in the attic, I made tea and served us both amid stacks of Van Ark's tepid art.

"Why would anyone go through the trouble of keeping all of this if he gave it up? He was cultured. He must have seen the writing on the wall. I can't imagine anyone wanting to save these for posterity."

Lee coughed into the crook of her arm.

"People sometimes create just to create. Art isn't always lofty. Sometimes it's just a nice painting or a good story, dearheart."

"Still, one has to wonder. Until he started to go crazy with jealousy, he had everything: a good business, wealth, and apparently the love of his life. Art is usually reserved for those who need more."

Lee turned and touched my arm. Her nose was running.

"That is probably the most pompous thing I've ever heard you say. You don't know what Van Ark wanted out of life. Besides, this is fun, and I plan to stay here until the smell drives me out. Go and write something." Her laugh lines crinkled momentarily.

"Are you catching cold, Lee? You sound hoarse. It's probably the mold from Van Ark's oeuvre."

"Go and write."

I climbed down the ladder and took a nap in the writing room.

+

The wind was cooler now. Summer was drifting away. Hannah Lee had been in my life for almost a year.

"Any more words?"

"Tomorrow. I'm not finished with the revisions."

"You used to let me see the first draft right away."

"Tomorrow, Lee. Can't we just walk on the beach and enjoy each other?"

The writing came in spurts, just enough to enliven our relationship for a week. After I finished a short story, the white house was alive and Miles' mournful trumpet echoed from the hallway. Most mornings however, I napped in the writing room and crammed my slight creative energy into the hours when Lee tended bar. Her own work had taken a disturbing turn as well. Three oil paintings of the Virgin Mary holding the still body of Christ lined the walls of Lee's workroom.

I stopped eating at the Maidenhead. I couldn't bear the familiarity Lee had with the pathetic men who drank their wages away night after night. I prepared candlelight dinners complete with a bottle of wine for Lee who indulged herself once in a while. I would occasionally lift a glass; I had no fear of backsliding. I understood what God had given me.

But as fall encroached, Hannah Lee grew listless, and entire dinners would go by with her doing nothing more than moving food around her plate. When I woke on the coach in the writing room, Lee was usually still asleep. She stopped buying the fashions she treated herself to as rewards upon completing a painting. The green mug lay broken in the sink. We went long stretches without touching each other even when we slept. The stack of books by our bed grew dusty, and when I returned them to the shelves, Lee said not a word.

On Lee's birthday, I presented her with an old hardbound set of the compete works of Mark Twain. While Lee slept through the afternoon, I cooked lobsters and baked a cake.

"I thought we could read them aloud to each other. Work our way through the whole darn thing."

"I need *your* words."

"Tomorrow. I might have something tomorrow."

"God gave you this talent, and you're wasting it by doting on me. Endlessly."

Lee's hand shook when she lifted the glass of wine to her mouth. It was as if the goblet was made of stone.

"Did your husband make dinners for you like this?"

"I need words to live."

"I baked a cake," I said as I left the table for the kitchen. When I returned, Lee was gone. Her lobster remained uneaten.

I climbed the stairs and paused in the doorway of the writing room. My father's desk was a mess, papers scattered here and there. Dust had overtaken the typewriter. There was nothing to write. I was fulfilled with Hannah Lee. Surely this was what God had intended for me. My life was a clear path. My writing led to financial independence, the death of my parents to a realization of God's intentions, the search for perfection through my art to Hannah Lee. I had nothing more to say.

Lee was curled beneath the blankets staring at Van Ark's fingers twisted around Lola's. The Jack Kerouac postcard was gone; I didn't remember when it had fallen or where it had gotten to. Lee was shivering.

"I just wanted you to have a nice birthday."

Lee pulled back the blankets, and I slid next to her, shoes still on my feet.

"I only wanted one thing."

"Me too. I only need you."

I stared at her face and tried to remember the last time her laugh lines emerged. It seemed so long ago. I kissed her mouth, and her breath was dry and thick with sleep even though she had only been in bed a few minutes.

"I only want one thing."

"Anything."

"Tell me a story," Hannah Lee asked, and I couldn't.

+

Lee was still asleep when I crawled into the attic with the crowbar from my car. The plywood crate stood on edge. We had been unable to open it. I was sure this would revive Lee. I found purchase along one side, and after a short struggle and about a dozen splinters, the lid pried open and split with a crack.

"Lola."

Lee was kneeling behind me, her nightgown draped over her bones. I hadn't heard her climb the ladder.

"You should put something on. It's damp up here."

Lee's eyes were wide and unmoving.

"No. Lola," she said pointing.

The first painting was a large oil of a comely Irish face in semi-profile, curly red hair grazing bare shoulders, blue eyes captured in a look of adoration. The strawberry birthmark was on her left cheek. It was the only flaw on an otherwise perfect face. The painting behind it was of the girl in the same pose with only the slightest differences. The next was also similar except Lola's eyes were dimmer, as if she'd tired of sitting and the artist, out of respect, had injected her impatience and boredom into the final product. There were nine more paintings of Lola, all in identical pose, the same white dress revealing her bare shoulders. In each one, Lola's face grew steadily paler, the look in her eyes developed from a glare into feral anger. The last painting was of a clearly terrified young girl, her eyes focused away from the artist as if toward a door or a window, any exit behind him.

Lee noticed it first, and only after I studied each painting in order twice through did the full picture become clear in my mind. In each portrait, the strawberry birthmark faded slightly, becoming a mere blemish until the final piece where it was gone altogether.

"He was a monster. Look at that poor girl's face," she sniffled.

I understood everything that Hannah Lee could not.

"No. He was trying to make her perfect. Van Ark wanted her to rise above the mud. He wanted to be remembered. He rose above his art."

"Lock them up. Put them back in the crate. He was a monster pure and simple."

Hannah Lee descended the ladder, and I replaced the lid on the crate. Although he had lost control at the end, Van Ark had struggled to immortalize Lola and therefore himself. Van Ark couldn't handle the task at hand, and Lola had been destined to be an old wives tale held dear by the fishermen for her surrender to the sea. I understood everything.

I swept my father's desk clean and put a Miles Davis record on the turntable. The white piece of paper overtook even my peripheral vision, and I surrendered to it.

In the morning, I rose on my own.

+

The story began as a simple one like they always do for me, gathering meaning and depth as the number of words grew: *Miller is a painter, an artist obsessed, as all true artists are, with the truth. His relative success affords him certain luxuries, and he is able to maintain a stable, well-equipped home for himself and his wife, a dark-haired creature who encourages his work and indulges the lengths to which he goes to be true to his art. When his wife buys a number of religious oils, Miller becomes fascinated with the look on Christ's face during His crucifixion and initiates, as his next undertaking, a study of the visage of death. His early attempts are abject failures. Undaunted, he haunts bars far from his own neighborhood and picks fights with the locals, rushing home to sketch the dazed look of fear on his face; using a mirror, he details his injuries and the dilation of his pupils. The mirror is his tool, and he cuts his arm repeatedly with a razor to see if his face registers the loss of blood. Miller videotapes himself masturbating—just his face. He turns the heat off in winter and still nothing comes close. His wife tends to his needs and continually strokes the flames of his artistic desire, remaining stoic throughout her husband's quest.*

"I'm sick. Can you make me some tea? It's so cold in here."

I made the tea but my mind was elsewhere. I wanted to feel Hannah Lee's body under mine.

"Not now. I'm sick."

"I need you, Lee."

Lee submitted, and when I finished, I headed back to Miller's story.

Miller begins imagining his wife is nailed to a cross when they make love. The sex is violent, but his Hezza understands where this is going and rubs his head as he cries himself to sleep. Miller finds himself in hardware stores looking at wood. He unearths a railroad spike in an abandoned train yard and impales a rabbit he bought at a pet store.

"The room is spinning. Make it stop." Lee was in bed again; she hadn't left it for two days.

"I want you to quit your job. I have more than enough money. Your husband may have needed you to work, but it's not necessary. Look at how strung out you are."

Miller contemplates the duality of Christ: if Jesus hadn't chosen to be sacrificed, if He hadn't accepted His Father's will, would his face have looked different? There is no doubt Jesus the man suffered unimaginable pain, but was it countered by Christ the Son of God? What would the countenance of a man driven to His death by His Father look like? Miller steels himself with a shot of whiskey, and with the mirror and video camera in place, drives a Swiss Army knife through his hand. Hezza unravels and leaves her husband, only to return to him as he recovers. Still, she is overcome with doubt.

"I need a doctor." It was the third day of writing, and Lee called from the bedroom. Red spots stained her cheeks from where she had scratched herself with her nails. She looked like a little girl beneath the blankets.

"I'm almost done, Lee. I'll have words for you."

"Oh God, there's not enough time. Take me to the doctor's."

"I know. I know. It's like there's not enough time for all the words, Lee."

Hezza calls a priest and asks him to visit the painter in their home. They discuss Christ's face at the moment of crucifixion. The white-haired priest tells Miller that he believes divine art comes from knowing God, from faith. He instructs the painter to internalize the face of God, to repeat His name over and over until He is at home in the heart.

"That's what prayer is, lad," says the priest, his pipe dangling in the corner of his mouth, "it's internalizing God. Communion is just the acting out of the internalization. Melville wrote 'you cannot hide the soul,' and no stronger words of truth do I know. Religious art—art that praises God—is the external tip of all that captures your soul."

When the priest leaves, Hezza touches Miller's arm and swears she will never leave him again; she will aid him in finding his truth no matter what the cost. Miller knows what he has to do.

Lee moaned from our bed. Her face was gaunt, and the red splotches had grown black with pus. "You have blood on your hands."

"It's just ink, Lee. It's almost done."

Miller buys some wood and begins constructing a large cross in the finished basement of their home. Over and over, he repeats God's name. For this I will be remembered, he thinks, I praise Him in my search for perfection. When his hands begin to tremble, Hezza helps him drive the nails to finish the cross.

Lee screamed from our bedroom.

I was bent over white paper, and although my mouth was dry and my stomach rumbled with hunger, I could not tear myself away.

Lee cried out my name.

Miller pours the wine and after a few glasses asks Hezza to pose on the cross. Hezza submits; the wine has made her pliant and proud of her husband. Miller lashes her arms with rope made of silk and binds her feet.

Lee's voice had become hoarse and soft. Her cries sounded like Billie Holiday.

I allowed myself to raise pen from paper. How great is God? So great that He rekindled my life's work when I had been blinded. My words praise Him, I thought; they are my gift to Him. Through my words, I will be remembered.

Hezza giggles under the influence, and Miller sets up his easel and chair, mixing his paints, cleaning his brushes.

"This will only hurt a second," Miller says to his wife.

"Said the spider to the fly," Hezza responds.

My parents' sacrifices will not be in vain, I thought, nor will Lee's faith in me. I was in the midst of creating a story of near perfection, a paragraph or two away from being in Hannah Lee's arms and nursing her back with my words. Beneath a rock, high atop every tree, even in the paintings of Van Ark's Lola, God is there guiding my hand.

Miller pats the towel next to his easel. He had bought the nails after spending an afternoon in the hardware store measuring them and feeling their weight. The hammer is new too. Hezza will be immortalized. Over and over he repeats God's name.

Lee gurgled and then fell silent.

+

I can tell you now that I tried to put the pen down. I can explain that in the course of detailing Miller's cross, I lost sight of what God wanted me to do. But words would be meaningless; they would be just words and everything has its price. Even faith. I can tell you all these things and more, but I did not comprehend what He was asking me to do until far too much ink had been spilled upon the page.

Miller drives the first nail into Hezza's left wrist, and the blood squirts on his face. He wipes it off with a clean towel and pauses to drink hot tea. Dirty work, this, he thinks.

No, I thought, He cannot ask me to sacrifice Hannah Lee. He promised her to me in a dream. He led me to this beach of honey to wed with her, to join our bodies into one. I created her with His hand guiding mine. Surely there must be some mistake. This He cannot ask of me.

I can tell you now how I tried to push the chair from the desk, but I would be lying. I knew how God worked. I understood His will. I raised my pen above the page. His will be done.

Miller pays no attention to his wife's shrieks; rather he times the exhalations in measured bars, all the while repeating God's name even while he plunges a spear into Hezza's side.

I can tell you now I believed God to be merciful. I can tell you the story of Abraham and Isaac on Mount Moriah. But I cannot wipe the ink from my hands.

Hannah Lee screamed once more. I heard the typewriter clack from the little table beside me. I closed my eyes. I think she screamed my name.

Miller smiles his way through the trial and continues to smile in jail. He thinks of his final painting and smiles. He even smiles when he takes out his own eyes.

+

The doctor said Hannah Lee died of a heart attack.

"By the look on her face, she was frightened to death. Maybe a nightmare. She died of fear."

I told the doctor nothing. I did not mention His name.

I arrived home from the hospital and sealed our bedroom with a padlock. I climbed the attic stairs and hid my story in the plywood crate with Lola, hammering it shut with two hundred nails.

I tried to fall asleep, but my body trembled itself awake every few minutes. Instead, I cleared my father's desk of pens and paper and pencils. I burned them in the kitchen sink. When I went upstairs to rid myself of the typewriter, I saw the paper sticking out from beneath the carriage.

"*...and then he let her go.*"

I knew what I had to do.

+

It was Deep Autumn, and the wind carried sea spray that felt like bee stings. On the jetty, I placed the typewriter on a slanted rock and knelt before it. Waves shook the rocks, but I no longer had fear. I typed without feeling the wind cut into my skin. I sang and tried to make my voice sound like Miles' trumpet. When the rain started, I was so drenched from the ocean I barely noticed.

"*...and then he let her go.*"

"*Are these words for me?*"

"*My name is Hannah Lee. Everyone calls me Lee.*"

"*You're walking me home, aren't you?*"

"*Say my name.*"

The wind carried my papers away, and the rain made the ink run. I can tell you I stayed on Lord's Finger until the light fought back the sky. I can tell you I wrote through the night. I can tell you all this, but I could not bring her back. He had won. Hannah Lee was gone.

+

This is the end of the story, my last. I alone stood witness to His folly, and now it is before you. My neighbors think me mad, and they would not be far from the truth. No further than I.

But sometimes during Deep Autumn, I watch a woman's outline against the place where the ocean kisses the sky. Sometimes she sings or recites a poem. Sometimes she dives into the water. And sometimes I join her, and we dance to the edge of Lord's Finger.

-end-

Redemption Stories

Backseat Love

"I'm sailing on this terrible ocean
I've come for myself to retrieve."
Sinéad O'Connor, "A Perfect Indian"

Recommended Soundtrack:

"A Perfect Indian" by Sinéad O'Connor

"Seasons In The Sun" by Terry Jacks

"Backseat Love" by Lola and the Shivers

my backseat love,
let's forget all about
the sound of the waves,
"just do what i say,"
but it's over my head
and i'm drifting away
like a promise made in the dark.

my backseat love,
while you fumble about,
your hand on my thigh:
"the water's too high."
it's a brother-love dare
to jump in the sky,
reflecting wide eyes to the air.

     i'll let you take off my dress
     if you promise to drive them away:
     the thoughts, they swirl, they choke,
     they crash to the shore...

my backseat love,
with your breath in my ear,
the hairs on my arms,
they danced with the waves.
"i'll pretend that i'm dead,
and float 'til i'm saved,
like a song that's stuck in your head."

my backseat love,
i hear your heart pound,
like mine on the day
i believed when he said:
"like my head to a gun,
and nothing will change,"
his face a squint in the sun.

     i'll let you take off my dress
     if you promise to drive me away;
     the dive, the swim, i choked,
     i bent to his will...

Absalom

"FAITH TAKES PRACTICE," said Owen Meany.
John Irving, *A Prayer for Owen Meany*

Recommended Soundtrack:

"Take Me Back" by Van Morrison

"Formula, Cola, Dollar Draft" by Marah

"Instant Karma"
by John Lennon and the Plastic Ono Band

roses grew wild there,
on the side of the house where you were born;
crawling to a place where the roof meets the sky,
torn, but not wasted, were the roots they left behind

    you said, "don't look too far behind,
    you don't want anyone, anyone to follow;
    let god paintbrush the night,
    and let the day be ours…"

well, the son you raised
had a boy of his own, and then, grandma,
he forgot everything 'bout where he was born;
thought scratching was what the ground was meant for

    you said, "don't look too far behind,
    you don't want anyone, anyone to follow;
    let god paintbrush the night,
    and let the day be ours…"

oh, he can't touch me now,
let alone believe what's become of me;
I'm far and away in places he'll never find;
torn, far from wasted, were the roots he left behind

        I
         denied
          all
           that
            exists
             within
              myself

    you said, "don't look too far behind,
    you don't want anyone, anyone to follow;
    let god paintbrush the night,
    and let the day be ours…"

O, the Burning of the Leaves

"One of these mornings, you're gonna rise up singing."
Janis Joplin & Big Brother and the Holding Company,
"Summertime"

Recommended Soundtrack:

"Maybelline" by Chuck Berry

"Strangers in the Night" {live version} by Jimmy Roselli

"Mystery Train" by Elvis Presley

"Summertime"
by Janis Joplin & Big Brother and the Holding Company

I stood beneath Lucky Joe's balcony and threw pennies up at his window. Some bounced off balcony rust; others trickled in the rain gutter like drunks coming out of McCullough's. A few pinged off the window dirt and flew back on me and Josie and Larry standing in the alley. I could hear "Maybellene" from a passing car on Saul Street. My aim was off, and we wanted some pictures from Lucky Joe.

"That's my last penny, Rose."

"I got it this time."

"Maybe he ain't home."

"He's home, Jo. Lucky Joe's always home."

"Oh shit. That was my last penny, Rose."

"Just take one of mine. Stop whining like a girl."

Flakes of dirt rained down, and there was Lucky Joe.

"Open it all the way, Lucky Joe."

"Hey, Lucky Joe!"

"Throw down some of those pennies, Lucky Joe."

Lucky Joe was always half silhouette, and he never came out to play. He was our age I guess, and we always went to him for pictures.

"Hi fellas. Sure making a racket out there! What kind of pictures do you need today?"

That was Lucky Joe. Always talking like a movie: *sure making a racket out there!* He used to make me stand under the window every Saturday afternoon and detail every frame of every feature, every cartoon, every preview. He never came out to play, but he went to the movies every Saturday through me.

"I was thinking about a train, Lucky Joe. Can you draw me a train? One that never stops but goes on and on. Something continental?"

I could hear Jimmy Roselli singing of lost love in Neapolitan behind Lucky Joe. Lucky Joe's mother must have loved Mr. Roselli; she played him all the time.

"I was thinking about an ape."

"Shut up, Larry."

"No, you shut up, Jo."

"Well, can you do a train, Lucky Joe? A big one?"

"For you, Rosebaby, anything!"

We waited across the street and sat on the old blue car near the opening of the alley. Larry wanted to see if he could spit clear across to the far wall but only managed to soil his shirt instead. I could see the sun slowly getting ready to take leave, and there would be hell to pay if I was late for supper, but I didn't want to rush Lucky Joe. I knew, even then, these things took time. Larry tried to spit again and Josie smacked him one. Across the way, dirt shimmied off glass as Lucky Joe stuck half his head past a curtain stained various shades of yellow.

"Done!"

I ran beneath the window, and Lucky Joe took one last look and floated the picture down. It was a train all right—mighty and sooty black. This train stopped for no one. If you weren't already on board, it passed you by like a bad dream, just pieces of it lingering after in your mind, a faint smell of coal in your nostrils. It was like that song: *"Well, that long black train, took my baby, and gone gone gone!"*

"That's great, Lucky Joe! Best yet!"

"Let me see, let me see."

"Larry, don't grab it out of her hand."

"For Christ's sake, don't tell me what to do, little girl."

"Don't curse at me, Larry Big Pants."

"I'll curse at who I want."

I ignored them both. The train fairly snorted off the page!

"It's really swell, LJ."

I knew he liked it when I called him LJ. I think it made him blush, but it was hard to tell from where I stood.

"Are you gonna hang it up, Rose?"

"You betcha! Right on the wall so when I'm lying in bed, it'll be like it's coming right toward me. *'Train a-rrive! Sixteen coaches long!'*

The song echoed in the alley, and Larry held his ears. My mother told me my singing was damn near a mortal sin. I liked to sing, but I couldn't carry a tune like Lucky Joe could draw a train.

"You got a great voice, Rosebaby."

"Save it, Ace. Gotta run home for supper. I'll come by on the weekend if I can."

"Wait, Rose. Aren't you gonna tell me a movie? Like in trade for the train?"

"I can't today...no, don't be sore. I'll be back, okay? And I'll tell you about everything I saw."

"Here's looking at you, kid!"

But I knew I wouldn't be back soon; it was late August, and high school loomed around the next bend, which meant a long bus ride, more homework, and a new batch of friends. I gave Lucky Joe a wiseass backward glance and blew him a kiss. Larry stopped giving Josie an Indian burn long enough to pick up all the pennies, his and ours. I grabbed Josie's hand and took off down the alley.

"Hey wait up! Why does he always talk like that?"

"Bye, Lucky Joe."

"Bye, LJ. Thank yoooooouuuu!"

"Why does he always talk like that?"

"Shut up, Larry."

"No, you shut up, Jo."

"Good-bye, Lucky Joe, good-bye! Good-bye, Lucky Joe, good-bye!"

+

My father was a joker. His love of laughter was second only to his joy at hearing someone else's. When I burst through the back porch door, he scooped me up and waltzed me across the kitchen linoleum.

"*Da la da da da, strangers in the night, la da da da da, strangers in the night.*"

"Daddy, stop it! You're crushing Lucky Joe's train."

"*Exchanging pictures, strangers in the night.*"

"Both of you, stop it."

"Come on, Mother, join your handsome man and his lovely daughter in a dance."

"You see I'm cooking, Harry. You're supposed to be chopping up the t-bone."

"Look at the picture Lucky Joe drew, Daddy."

"Sure, baby."

"Rose, you stop taking things from that retarded child."

My father knelt down and gazed into the picture so long I thought he was going to fall into it. A staccato of laughs escaped him. My mother's back stiffened. I could smell tomato gravy from where she stood facing the stove.

"That train is a moose, Ro, a real moose."

"A train can't be a moose, Daddy!"

"Sure it can. Ain't you ever heard of a cabmoose?"

"That's it, you no-good-son-of-a-bitch. Either chop that meat or get out of my kitchen."

My mother was fond of the phrase "no-good-son-of-a-bitch," particularly to describe my father, whom she saw as being too Irish and thus too easy going when it came to us kids and life in general I guess. I could never picture her young and beautiful, just weary and cranky. My father was never too tired to be my racehorse in the hallway or my teammate in wire ball.

He seized the colander from the drainer and wore it as a hat.

"All aboard now!"

His brogue turned into a midwestern accent.

"Next stop, Chopmeat City!"

Mother snatched the colander (and a good handful of his thinning whites). My throat hurt from swallowed laughter.

"Get out of my goddamn kitchen, you no-good-son-of-a-bitch! And take your little playmate too."

"Now, Margaret, don't be taking the good Lord's name in vain…"

She swung at his head with the wooden spoon, and he picked me off the floor. Mother turned her back on us, still muttering, and Father undid her apron strings with his free hand before we both escaped through the western-style swinging doors.

"Don't mind your mother, baby. I woke her up this morning, don't you know?"

My father loved to wake my mother up! My mother on the other hand, valued sleep like prayer. She even forced my father to sleep in the room I shared with Margie when his snoring grew too loud, or on the couch if he had been drinking and playing cards with Uncle Bucky or Hap from across the street. My father had ingenious ways of rousing my mother. Sometimes he would start singing in that awful voice of his from inside of the closet. Once he threw a baseball through an open bedroom window and then ran in the kitchen and sat at the table pretending to read his paper and eat his Quaker Oats. Mother came downstairs in her floor length cotton nightgown and, without a word, plopped the baseball into Father's oatmeal. I'll never forget the admiring look on his face. He fairly beamed!

Another time he crawled under the bed and tried to lift it with his back while on his hands and knees. Mother bolted out of bed and met with a closed door. She broke her collarbone and that wasn't so funny. My father took off from work and stayed with her every day at the hospital, waiting on her while she convalesced. But it didn't stop him. He loved to wake her up, and she loved to complain and bite at him.

"The picture, Daddy. I left Lucky Joe's train in there."

I said "there" like you would say "haunted house." I didn't hate my mother, but I sure as hell didn't want to be around her too long.

"Don't worry now, Ro-Ro. I'll rescue the train."

Father whipped Mother's afghan off the back of the sofa and wrapped it around him like a cape.

"Daddy? Why can't Lucky Joe come out and play like everyone else? What's wrong with him? Everyone says stuff like he's contagious or has three legs, but what's really wrong?"

He knelt on one knee and I crawled on his back. I could smell the wood chips in his hair from work.

"Well, baby, it isn't like your dear momma says. Lucky Joe isn't retarded or even contagious; he doesn't have three legs. Fact is he doesn't have any legs, Ro. Yes, that's the truth. There was a car accident, and his father died in the wreck, and the wreck took Lucky Joe's legs. His poor mother. God. Can't imagine."

He swung his arms behind him and hugged me hard. I buried my face in the red folds of his neck.

"She took to drink in a bad way, baby. Real bad. She doesn't come out of the house either to tell the truth. I think she even has her groceries delivered. She used to be a friend of your dear momma's and a member in good standing with the Sons of Italy, but now, well, she just hides up there and hides him too."

"That's not fair, is it, Daddy? Couldn't Lucky Joe get a wheelchair or something?"

"I don't know, baby. I guess. Best not to dwell on it."

I climbed off my father's back.

"Sure can draw, can't he though? The good Lord saw it fit that he could hold a pencil right, don't you know?"

I noticed my father's empty glass behind the octagon side table. I liked getting my father a drink. I picked up the glass and stole an ice cube.

"Can I freshen your drink, sir?"

"If you can do it without your mother seeing you near the liquor cabinet, then sure. In the meantime, I'll rescue your picture from the hands of the evil one."

Quickly I tumbled whiskey over remains of ice and replaced it behind the octagon table. I could hear my mother yelling at my father: "...get out of the g.d. trash...are you an animal, Harry?...get out now...have you been drinking while I've been...?"

And on and on. My mother wasn't evil; she wasn't even that

mean really. She was, in a word, superstitious. A robin landed once on the kitchen windowsill where Mother cooled the pies, and my sister and I missed school for a week. Turns out no one died, but Mother dutifully read aloud all the obits over breakfast. Margie, who wasn't as smart as me, thought we were praying for the lost souls like when the priest reads out the remembrances in church. Margie would Hail Mary out loud, Mother would smack the top of her head for interrupting her, and Father and I would turn red from hiding the giggles.

It made sense that Mother would throw Lucky Joe's train in the trash. She trashed his picture like she trashed his name, like it was bad luck to know him.

Father emerged with the picture and a huge tomato gravy grin.

"Better hang this up now, baby. I spilled some sauce, and she's about to move on to the meatballs! Now, hurry down and tell me one of your stories."

I tacked the picture across from my bed and scurried back down the stairs. My mother disapproved of made-up stories, but my father reacted to mine as if they were part of the Bible itself.

I spun a new tale and kept talking until Mother yelled it was time for supper.

+

I was laying half in bed and half out, trying like hell to adjust the Mary, Mother of God, night light so the virgin's rays would shine on Lucky Joe's train. It took me an hour, and by then even Margie, who never shut up, finally did and fell asleep. I dreamed of all the places it would take me, of the grand train that would bring me home in triumph and the parade they would have for Rose the scribbler, Rose the novelist, Rose the top-notch journalist who braved war and lions and Russian spies to capture a story!

My father came in our room. He was trying to be quiet, but he stepped on a bear that spoke when his tummy was pushed.

"Shit."

"Someone's been eating my porridge."

"Shhhh. Margie's asleep, Daddy."

"Damn."

"Someone's been sitting in my chair."

"Sorry, baby."

Father sat on the edge of my bed and played with my hair. His whiskey breath was like a second blanket.

"Just checking on you girls before I turned in."

"It's the couch tonight, Daddy?"

"Lucky it's not the shed, baby."

"You're lucky it's not the train tracks."

We both laughed quietly as to not wake Margie.

"Listen, baby, about Lucky Joe: don't pay attention to any of your dear momma's bullshit. Everyone has something to offer. Lucky Joe too."

My father slurred his words around the whiskey; he was up to his nipples in drink!

"Just don't be a taker, Ro. Make sure you give back. Make sure you give back. Now listen, it's important you give back."

"Shhh, Daddy. I understand already: give back."

"That's the bone truth. Spring appears and everything comes alive. Fall arrives and those same things die. The truth is: there is no truth; it's only what you make of the time in between."

My father's silhouette on the wall, the profile of his nose, the way he stared at his callused hands when his voice turned down what Margie called Serious Street: I remember thinking my father was a wonderful song trapped in my head all the day long.

"Everyone goes it alone, okay? You go alone. Nothing goes with. Nothing except the love you give back. Nothing except the love you goddamn give back."

"Okay, Daddy. Nothing except the love you goddamn give back."

That caught him off guard and set him coughing.

"What is it? Do we have to get up for school?"

"Go back to sleep, Margie. Daddy's just checking on us."

He stepped on a few more bears and assorted animals and kissed Margie's head of curls good-night and then came back to my bed to kiss mine.

"Now go to sleep, little ones. I love you both very much."

As he left the room, he grabbed the speaking bear (on its third round of "*Who's been sleeping in my bed?*") and managed a barely seen wink in the light of the Virgin Mary.

"Who's been peeing in his bed?"

"Go to sleep, Margie. It's nothing."

But it was far from nothing. It was my father's decidedly

awkward way of being a hero. My hero. I stared hard at the train, imagining my father and me on an exotic adventure, chasing a one-armed man or maybe a boy with no legs, the truth our quarry, until I fell asleep.

+

My father managed to wake my mother on the day he died. Of this final act, I am sure he was proud. I was in my early twenties and working not as an investigative reporter or the next Edith Wharton but as the clichéd, harried waitress. I had my own apartment, and about the only things I ever wrote were checks.

The phone rang a half dozen times that Saturday. I almost gave up. On the seventh ring, my father answered. It was nine in the AM, and he had already been at the liquor cabinet.

"Daddy, it's Rose."

"Ro-Ro! Where are my goddamn eggs? I ordered eggs hours ago."

"Stop it. I thought you were going fishing with Hap."

"Nope. That's what I told your mother. I'm going over Bucky's for poker later tonight. Gagliardi said he would give me time and a half under the table if I cleaned the warehouse this afternoon. Figured it would be my poker money. Don't tell your mother."

"I won't, Daddy. Just don't get caught."

"I'm a sinner, baby, don't you know?"

"Save it, Ace. I'm just calling to check on you."

"Got any stories for me?"

"Not unless charred meat loaf turns you on, no."

"Well, you better check on your mother too. I'll wake her!"

"No, Daddy!"

I heard a click a few moments later as he picked up the bedroom extension.

"Margaret! Wake up! It's our baby! On the phone!"

"No Daddy, don't."

"Why you no-good-Irish-son-of-a-bitch…"

"Bye, baby!"

I hung up too.

+

This is what happened:

Daddy walked to Bucky's when he finished working the Saturday shift. After two hands, he went to the bathroom. Twenty minutes passed. Bucky knocked on the door.

"You all right there, Harry?"

"Please. Come in, Buck. Help me."

He was half on the toilet and half off. My uncle helped him buckle up and went to call my mother and an ambulance.

"No, Buck. Just help me home."

Uncle Bucky helped my father, moving slowly and half bent, walk home all six blocks. It was October, Deep Autumn, and I'm sure they could smell the burning of the leaves. My father climbed into bed, expelled his bowels upon my mother's meticulously washed and wind dried sheets (six clothes pins, not four), and passed into a better world.

I moved back home and tried my best to take care of Mother. When she took to her bed (a new one; she had Bucky throw out the old one and had the new mattress placed in the guestroom), I quit waitressing and took up medicine doses and bedpans. When she took to throwing her bedpans at me whenever I tried to lighten the mood, I quit medicine doses and bedpans too. Margie was more like Mother than I was and a better suited companion too, according to Mother. I wanted wheels—I was always like that. I was ready to hit the road, Jack.

+

I stood beneath Lucky Joe's balcony and threw pennies up at his window. Some bounced off balcony rust; others trickled in the rain gutter like drunks coming out of McCullough's.

I didn't know if Lucky Joe still lived there. I didn't care either.

When the dirty window rattled open, I jumped back a step.

"Hi Rose. Sure making a racket out there! What kind of pictures do you need today?"

"I was thinking about a train, Lucky Joe. Can you draw me a train? One that never stops but goes on and on. Something continental?"

I strained to hear Mr. Roselli's singing, but all I heard was the trolley car on the Avenue and the sound the leaves make when they spiral into the wind.

After a while, Lucky Joe said:

"Seen any movies lately, Rose? Something good?"

I hadn't been to the movies since the 10th grade. I hadn't seen anything except the religious programs Mother watched on the old black and white. But I needed a picture in the worst way.

"Sure, Lucky Joe."

So I closed my eyes and made one up. I had almost forgotten how, but after a few false starts, I told Lucky Joe all about a steam train and some Irish spies and a treasure chest filled with pennies and a woman who tied herself to a bed and an old soldier who wore a cape and how a little boy trapped in a room ended up saving the day.

I talked for so long, the sun had stolen the day back, and I knelt in the shadows beneath Lucky Joe's window.

When I opened my eyes, the picture had been carried halfway down the alley by the breeze and Lucky Joe's window was closed tight. His drawing of the horizon took what little breath I had away. They seemed to go on forever, the rays of the sun, expanding into a hundred roads, a thousand train tracks.

For a moment my heart left with the leaves.

I threw my last pennies at Lucky Joe's window and watched them bounce off the railing, revealing black beneath rust. I caught one. It was warm in my palm. I gulped and hurled it back, cracking the window, making lines like a traced treasure map.

"Good-bye, Lucky Joe, good-bye! Good-bye, Lucky Joe, good-bye!"

I tucked the picture into my sleeve, gave a wiseass backward glance, my last, and chased the remaining trails of the sun out of the alley and onto Saul Street. I was singing:

"*Train a-rrive! Sixteen coaches long! Well, that long black train took my baby and gone gone gone!*"

-end-

About the Author:

Michael-Patrick Timothy Harrington was born in Philadelphia, Pennsylvania and now lives in the suburb of Ambler. His childhood was fraught with terror, being forced to stay outside by his mother ("sun's out, you're out"), made to stay up way past bedtime by his grandmother Ro-Ro, and told to "eat it or wear it" by Aunt El. Michael-Patrick's mother lessened the blows by buying him his first 45s; he still has every single one of them. He wrote his first short story in 2nd grade, punched his sister Kathie in 3rd grade, grew peach fuzz on his upper lip in 5th or 6th grade, kissed a girl in 10th grade, but never broke any bones. In elementary school, Michael was hijacked by Tolkien and Twain and the Beatles and Hitchcock; he never recovered. After surviving Holy Ghost Preparatory School, Michael-Patrick attended La Salle University. There he was confronted by Hemingway and Fitzgerald and Faulkner and emerged deeply scarred (in a good way). It was around this time that the opposite sex became a conundrum; the problem persists today. Michael-Patrick has had a variety of jobs, including operating his own record store and owning or co-owning several mail order companies. He has played in the rock'n'roll bands Zen Arcade and Lola and the Shivers. He also found time to finish college, graduating Magna Cum Laude from Arcadia University. The author can frequently be found eating popcorn in a dark movie theater. Michael-Patrick is a vegetarian and enjoys the color green. *Deep Autumn* is Michael-Patrick's first book. Everything in it is false with a ring of truth. He's not in love. All interested parties should contact him immediately. Michael-Patrick is survived by his stuffed dog Woofer.

Contact Information
www.michaelpatrickharrington.com
e-mail: michael@michaelpatrickharrington.com